MW01713740

A.E. OSLER

# *Anatolian Spring*

Lorie –

I'm pleased and touched that you are sampling this Turkish tale of mine, and hope that you enjoy it.

Affectionate regards.

Alan – August 2009

Note for Librarians: A cataloguing record for this book is available from Library and Archives Canada at www.collectionscanada.ca/amicus/index-e.html
ISBN 1-4120-9146-2

*Printed in Victoria, BC, Canada. Printed on paper with minimum 30% recycled fibre. Trafford's print shop runs on "green energy" from solar, wind and other environmentally-friendly power sources.*

TRAFFORD PUBLISHING™
*Offices in Canada, USA, Ireland and UK*
This book was published *on-demand* in cooperation with Trafford Publishing. On-demand publishing is a unique process and service of making a book available for retail sale to the public taking advantage of on-demand manufacturing and Internet marketing. On-demand publishing includes promotions, retail sales, manufacturing, order fulfilment, accounting and collecting royalties on behalf of the author.

**Book sales for North America and international:**
Trafford Publishing, 6E–2333 Government St.,
Victoria, BC V8T 4P4 CANADA
phone 250 383 6864 (toll-free 1 888 232 4444)
fax 250 383 6804; email to orders@trafford.com
**Book sales in Europe**:
Trafford Publishing (UK) Limited, 9 Park End Street, 2nd Floor
Oxford, UK OX1 1HH UNITED KINGDOM
phone 44 (0)1865 722 113 (local rate 0845 230 9601)
facsimile 44 (0)1865 722 868; info.uk@trafford.com
**Order online at:**
trafford.com/06-0900

10 9 8 7 6 5 4 3 2 1

## Chapter 1

*Ephesus, Western Turkey*
*March, 1982*

TREVOR MALCOLM SAW that the man who had attacked him lay face down and inert between two toppled stones, his head in a halo of blood-soaked grass; looking as though he might have prostrated himself to pray or to drink from a hidden spring and fallen asleep. Warily watching, as the halo glistened and grew in the sunlight , he recalled his rage in the seconds before he'd lost consciousness, his horror at the senselessness of what was happening, his conviction that his life was about to end—incomprehensibly, meaninglessly; then he got to his feet unsteadily from all fours and stood tilting his face towards the sun. What was it he'd been doing, just before? He'd paused to sharpen his *conté* pencil, looked up from his almost finished sketch of the Street of the Merchants. The attack had come without warning, apparently provoked by nothing more than a greeting.

Seeing himself whittling at the fragile *conté* pencil, taking care not to break the point, he made with dismay the fatal connection between the small Swiss knife he still clutched in his right hand and the way the incident had concluded. He'd never let go of the knife; and with the fellow's fingers on his throat and the sky turning black before his eyes he'd thrust blindly, flailed wildly, until he'd fallen.

Things are not as one is led to believe, he reflected. Events of his past life had not flashed before him in those moments of near-death; there had been no pictures of the barefoot urchin in the Grampians, nothing to remind him of his lean school or university years, or of his disastrous marriage; any more than of certain discoveries which had, more recently, excited him and earned him some respect among his peers. Things are not as one is led to believe. A fellow creature, perfectly unknown to you, from whom you might expect a smile and a 'Good morning,' tries to kill you instead.

He leant shakily against the nearest of the huge broken stones forming the top gallery of the ancient Theatre of Ephesus and tried to focus on what lay below. Thankfully, the Theatre lay empty, its curving lines of seats grey ripples in an apparently unaccusing sea, frozen in their advance as they had been for centuries. His eye fell on three women beyond, starting up the Arcadian Way, on a group of boys throwing stones at a wall to hit lizards, on a party of Arabs idling before the Library of Celsus. How much time had passed? No matter; surely they—the women, the boys, the Arabs—would all have been too far away to have seen anything. They were simply getting on with what they were doing, as though nothing had happened.

Find out who the bastard was, he counseled himself.

He continued to wait, fearing someone would pop from behind one of the stones; but when after several minutes no one did he stepped to the body of the man and knelt. The blood, congealing now around the head and darkening the grass, brought nausea. He got to his feet and turned away, struck fully with the enormity of what he had done. Everything had changed—himself most of all, as though metamorphosed by some malevolent and invisible god of the place. Trevor Malcolm, formerly archaeologist; now killer. He struggled into his jacket to hide his blood-stained tee-shirt. He stooped and wiped his blood-sticky fingers and sketch-book on a patch of grass. What was he to do now, in the immediate present? All he knew was that he couldn't stay here a moment longer. Snapping shut the Swiss knife and thrusting it and the sketch-book into the shopping bag he'd brought his lunch in, he took several deep breaths, tried to slow his racing heart; then made for the path he knew about, the same path the man had climbed, which ran from the back of the Theatre down the hillside to the visitors' parking lot.

Through the humming of bees busy among the wild daisies and anemones there came on the soft spring air the slight, normally unremarkable, now significant, now ominous, sound of a car door slamming. He glimpsed a figure moving between the deep shadows of the stunted pines below and making for the path. Tensely, he descended. Moments later a man shouldered past him, wheezing as he climbed. Trevor Malcolm flung himself down the remaining slope. Had the man seen him, looked at him enough to remember him? He couldn't be sure; he hadn't dared lift his own eyes from the stones beneath his feet.

Not far from where the path ended and the pot-holed parking lot began sat an old yellow Mercedes estate car—belonging, perhaps, to the man of the path? Passing it at a distance, he glanced aside: no one in the Mercedes; only, some metres from it, a tall youth in dark glasses and a beret arguing with one of the tribe of local urchins who pester tourists to buy postcards and souvenirs.

At the far end of the parking lot he was rattled to hear someone shouting—a woman, calling out, hailing him in English. She had stepped from a little group of Turks and was waving frantically. A tourist who'd seen everything after all, he thought in panic. A damned tourist. But how was that possible? An instant later he saw his error: it was not that at all, she wanted something else, wanted help.

'Please!' she was saying. 'I think you must speak English!'

'Yes,' he snapped, strongly inclined to pretend he didn't. Apparently his Marks & Spencer bag had attracted her attention, given him away.

'There's been some darned misunderstanding,' she began breathlessly. 'I was with this tour—'

What had happened, he gathered, was that the tour bus she had been on had left without her. She was stranded, all alone, with little money and no passport. So he must see how desperate her situation was. A real godsend that he'd come along because she couldn't understand a word of Turkish. Not a single word.

He was in no mood to sympathize. He could scarcely look at her. She was a blurred object, an object very much in the way. He thought only of the man climbing the path, and of what the man would do when he saw the body lying among the stones. With barely concealed fury he agreed to escort her on the two kilometre walk to Selçuk, where she could catch a local *dolmush* to take her back to her hotel in Izmir. Beneath his breath he cursed her. The last thing he needed right now, when he was desperate to think what he ought to do next—whether he ought to hide himself or go to the police—was to get saddled with this obviously scatty female.

## Chapter 2

Carey Signorello stood in the company of a dozen dusky and inscrutable Turks, nervously awaiting the arrival of the *dolmush* that would take her back to Izmir; and pondering the mystery of why the tour bus, under the direction of Kadir, the guide, had abandoned her in the parking lot at Ephesus. Exasperated, she exchanged the question for another, one she had fleetingly entertained before: Why not take advantage of the situation and stay over to revisit Ephesus tomorrow morning? She'd prepared herself mainly for the Byzantine Christian churches of northern Greece, with their frescoes and icons—Mario's world. Ephesus had come as a surprise. She had responded slightly against her will to its atmosphere, the extent to which its architecture and marble streets enabled the imagination to resurrect life in pre-Christian times. She'd had no idea the ruined city was so intact, so vast and fascinating. And the tour this afternoon hadn't left her nearly enough time there. It would mean *overnight*, however; if she stayed, and how would she feel, alone in this foreign village, a village seemingly inhabited almost entirely by black-clad, moustached men, when darkness fell? She knew no one—except the stranger who had so truculently, disquietingly, escorted her here to this god-forsaken bus stop.

She couldn't remember what he'd called himself, whether it was Malcolm Trevor or Trevor Malcolm, but it had been while walking here with him that the idea of staying over had first come to her; and coincidentally, the very next moment, he—Malcolm Trevor or Trevor Malcolm—had brought it out, put it to her, tauntingly, and not dreaming, of course, that it would appear as quite such a challenge to her; since the idea drove like an Ottoman dagger to the heart of her sheltered, spoiled existence, jarred painfully with the cautious and calculating person she feared she had become, having lived for the last seven years a cosseted and numbingly comfortable life, the compliant and ostensibly contented wife of a strong-minded, generous, well-intentioned, older man. It was not his fault; and it was up to her to change. Yet the idea alarmed her, as representing upheaval, possibly calamity. It alarmed her, too, ambivilantly, as seeming to speak, or at least whisper, beguilingly, to a certain disquiet, a restlessness of a different sort, a vague yearning, she'd found herself half-heartedly, fitfully, fighting of late.

It was her fault, her fault entirely, if there was anything wrong; anything wrong between Mario and herself.

But it was, after all, out of the question. She couldn't be expected to stay over on the spur of the moment in a strange Turkish village, to take such a bold, spontaneous decision. For good or ill she wasn't the adventurous type. Not any more. She knew she wasn't; Mario knew she wasn't. And could she be expected to change from what she had become, at twenty-nine—though part of her might wish it?

To the stranger, who didn't know her, didn't know Mario, she was something else altogether. He'd made no allowances. His contempt had been palpable. And enraging. Clearly, he'd dismissed her as the predictable, run-of-the-mill tourist, the tourist in a hurry, the tourist with too much money and too little sensitivity, a caricature of the American abroad. She knew he'd never for a moment expected her to act on his suggestion, never expected her to stay the night in Selçuk in order to revisit the ruins and 'do them justice.' His suggesting what she had timidly, secretly, put to herself had been tongue-in-cheek, a taunt. Nothing remotely resembling an invitation, at any rate.

Yet leaving that aside it was a coincidence, and Carey tended to believe in the significance of coincidence.

The American tourist, the tourist in a hurry. Well, when she had hailed him in the parking lot at Ephesus she'd been in a panic rather than in a hurry, and to anyone with an ounce of understanding that panic would have drawn a sympathetic response. He'd met her breathless description of the disappearance of Kadir and the tour bus with a grunt of contempt. He'd let it be known he disapproved of people who go in for guided tours and view foreign countries through the tinted windows of a bus. He'd been intent on ignoring her altogether, on passing by without helping; and then during their walk he'd responded to her pleas, her questions, shortly, at times exasperatedly. He'd been offhand, rude. He'd tried in odd ways to antagonize her. He'd managed to add to her bewilderment, apparently deriving a perverse satisfaction by increasing her nervousness. Physical violence would not be beyond him, she surmised;

had they known each other better. How could I have offended him? she mused. How could I have? Stranded in the middle of nowhere through no fault of my own. Did he hate Americans? Was that it? Or was it because I gave him the impression I have money back at the hotel, saying I might take a taxi all the way to Izmir, or happening to mention the cruise ship that's taking us on next week from Istanbul to Greece?

Yes, money. My having money. He had a thing about money.

Yet his mind seemed to have been made up from the start. That was what made the thing even odder.

'I know it sounds stupid,' she'd explained breathlessly in the parking lot, 'but I've been left here by the bus I was on. Maybe you saw it, a big blue tour bus—'Aegean Sun Fun Tours.' If you'd tell me how to get back—'

'To?'

'Izmir. Back to Izmir. Where my hotel is. That's where the tour's gone. I don't even know how far—look, is there a town around here somewhere?'

'There—' he gestured sweepingly, only to wince with apparent pain. 'Ephesus. I've got to go—'

'But it's *dead*!' she wailed.

'So it is,' he said, absently now, his eyes travelling beyond her, as though the fallen stones, the olive and pine-clad hills, and especially the almost empty parking lot, were of greater moment. 'Dead from the mosquitoes.'

'*What*?'

'Mosquitoes.'

'Some town—?'

'Malarial mosquitoes. Got them in the end.'

Talking at cross-purposes. Could anyone be more infuriating? Talking now about mosquitoes!—'*Please*, is there a town where I can get to Izmir from?'

'Izmir's an hour and a half,' he grudgingly volunteered. 'There's a town called Selçuk just two kilometres along this road.'

'Kilometres? How far's that—in miles, I mean.'

He didn't answer, as if determined to further irritate or frighten her. He was ignoring her altogether, looking away again, with one hand raised to shade his eyes; his gaze sweeping the undergrowth surrounding the arches of the ancient gymnasium to their right, then veering back to the parking lot over her shoulder.

'How far?' she persevered. 'In miles.'

'One,' he snapped. 'One mile. A short walk. There's a bus stop as you get to the town.'

Well, that was something. 'Selçuk,' she repeated, only to have him turn abruptly. In alarm she saw he considered their parley at an end. She would be left alone. 'But *you're* walking that way, aren't you?' she protested, raising her voice at his back. 'Surely you won't mind if I—'

He walked quickly, thrusting his head and shoulders forward energetically so his legs seemed from moment to moment in danger of being left behind and of allowing the rest of him to pitch ahead to the ground. She had trouble keeping up, but dared not complain. Indignation, anger, bafflement, gusted through her; yet as she went further and became aware of her dependence on him, and of their isolation, she became more and more anxious. Could this be the same road the tour bus had taken, bringing her to Ephesus some three hours before? Was he leading her somewhere else, out of spite, or design? She recognised nothing. Perhaps because Gloria had been talking so much to her. Yaking, the whole way. The road lay flat before them, now, between the hills, flanked on either side by a line of leafless willows with whitewashed trunks. Further on she was only slightly relieved to see human figures. The willows were being trimmed. Branches lay across the road in places. Men in shirt-sleeves and black trousers, women in voluminous orange and red trousers with headscarves hiding their hair and tied beneath their chins, hauled away branches and swept the road clean. Some of the men stared, smiling, or raised a hand in greeting; while the women worked on oblivious. Branches were being dumped into carts, lashed over the backs of donkeys, or secured to bicycles. Large birds presided over all of this, half grey and half black, of a species she had not seen before; wary sentinels watching for she knew not what on either side of the road among the willows.

At one point, during their walk, he had done more than annoy her, more even than add to her anxiety; he had—briefly—terrified her. Bringing this vividly to mind, she shivered, now, almost as violently as she had then. Hearing a car approaching from the direction of Ephesus, she'd had the idea of a lift; but before the car neared them from around a bend he'd clutched her arm and tugged her behind the line of white-washed willows bordering the road, snarling that he didn't want to be seen—but offering, as they walked on, no further explanation.

I'm on a road somewhere in the middle of Turkey, she had told herself incredulously, moments after this event; following a stranger, a man who must have done something wrong, God knows what, a thoroughly disagreeable individual in any case; and I'm without my passport!

Being without her passport was an added cause for alarm. Her American passport. Showing the world who she was, where she belonged. She had known she would not be needing it that day to cross any frontier or cash a travellers' cheque; still, she'd been a fool to leave it back at the Izmir Palas, zipped up in the side pocket of her suitcase.

'You were at the far end of the parking lot,' broke from him suddenly. It was like a jab. He had halted and spun round without warning, so she slightly—yet electrifyingly—collided with him. 'You wouldn't have noticed who was near the hill, the hill they call Mount Pion, and the path I came down?'

'No, I—'

'The path—'

'Path—' she repeated stupidly.

'A man taking the path up the hill I came down, who I think was from a yellow Mercedes estate parked there, the one that passed us just now; and nearer you a kid in a beret talking with a boy?' When she shook her head at all of this he turned impatiently and resumed walking. Minutes later, when she had resigned herself, half gratefully, to a moody truce that had fallen between them, he startled her again; this time in a different tone, with: 'You say you got left behind by your tour bus. How the hell did you manage that?'

'I haven't any idea,' she responded. 'Can't figure it out.'

She caught up briefly and managed to glare aside at him. Not that he took any notice. But really, she was beyond caring much about what he said or thought. She only wanted to be safely at the bus stop, reassured there would be a bus going to Izmir.

'It's a shock,' she said after a time, wanting suddenly, obscurely, to be more accepted, 'being stranded like this. I don't even have my passport. It's not a country women should travel alone in, is it?'

'Oh, why not? Afraid you'll be stuffed into a sack and dumped in a harem?'

'No!' she protested. 'That sort of thing doesn't go on any more!'

He said nothing.

'I think you're *mean* to suggest it,' she could not help blurting. 'Purposely mean. You have been all along. Why are you being like that?' She regretted her words at once; she was furious with herself for wanting to understand.

Trevor Malcolm had strode on, pretending not to hear.

Now, at the bus stop, she dwelt on the oddness of the encounter, while telling herself the last thing in the world she wanted was to find some excuse for the man. She shuddered, recalling how they had trudged together for twenty minutes or so; he keeping always a stride or two ahead, as though to be rid of her the sooner; she, warily, indignantly, flustered, following in the wake of his unaccountable perturbation.

But she must put him out of her mind. I don't need any of this, she told herself. Not on top of jet lag and everything else.

'Everything else' really boiled down to what she deemed she had become in seven years of marriage. She meant her own inadequacy. She had faded, somehow—in her own estimation; and, she had begun to suspect, in Mario's. Not in beauty, but in energy, enthusiasm, vital force. She couldn't remember when she had last moved her husband to make love to her. With the prospect of this trip had come the notion that she might return to him improved—worthy of him, and the position he'd made for himself, the respect he'd won; return more exciting, with new things to say, a new outlook on life and on herself. Except that more and more of his time seemed taken up by his business and other people, the clients and friends who flocked around him and who had to be elaborately catered for, Mario was the ideal husband. She was the luckiest woman in the world to have found him, or to have been found by him. And that was another thing: she would return from this trip newly appreciative, even more grateful.

Good, kind, Mario. She saw him, waving good-bye to her at JFK, where he had insisted on escorting her, despite being so busy. Waving good-bye, blowing her a kiss. She would think about him, often; and send him thought-messages. (She believed in telepathy, and considered herself gifted that way.)

All at once she wanted desperately to stay over; for *his* sake, paradoxically.—I *should* change, she told herself. And perhaps I could, by not being so timid, so predictable, all the time.

From where she stood among the little crowd at the bus stop she could make out *Otel Croesus*, in faded lettering, set in the crumbling plaster of what the stranger had said was the town's only hotel. The front of the building appeared to have wedged itself into the partially ruined arches of an aqueduct. Quaint, but not necessarily civilized. Obviously not the Hilton. It wasn't even in her Fodor, she'd seen moments ago. For that matter the town, Selçuk, didn't rate a separate heading there, earning merely passing mention as the modern town nearest Ephesus. Tourists weren't expected to stay here; they streamed off their cruise ships alongside the Club Med at Kusadasi or the quays at Izmir, to be sped by bus to Ephesus and the other archaeological sites that dotted the coast of Aegean Turkey. But she was here, now, dumped unaccountably in Selçuk. And notwithstanding her wariness or prudence or sense of proleptic guilt, the idea of returning to Ephesus at leisure and strolling around the ruins on her own tempted her. This much, at least, she would acknowledge. Archaeology had once been her passion—before the *agrémens* incident upon Mario's wealth had turned her from the paths of serious study. (It wasn't his fault. He'd remained blithely unaware of that and other effects his money had had on her.) But she could think of herself as an archaeologist *manqué*, and here she might even pretend—

Across the road and down it some fifty yards: the Hotel Croesus. She had only to ask for a room. Someone would speak English. And there would be no difficulty about accommodating her, the season having not properly begun. The hotel probably stood quite empty—except for the puzzling stranger, with whom she need have nothing to do.

*Yes*, she told herself. She would stay. Her heartbeat accelerated at the idea. I'll check in, then buzz the Izmir Palas, leave a message for Kadir saying I'll rejoin the tour tomorrow evening. It had rained earlier and the sky still looked uncertain, but she remembered Kadir saying the weather was set to improve. Tomorrow would be warmer, more spring-like. She had her Dental Floss, her Tylenol, just enough Turkish money.

No sooner had she made up her mind on the subject than a stab of fear caused her to change her mind.

Mario's assurances notwithstanding, she'd formed the impression that Turkey was a dangerous country. She knew that terrorist attacks and assassinations had been followed by a military takeover. But did the soldiers make it better? At the airport in Izmir she had seen them, all looking alike, as though cloned from one brutal original, with their dead eyes and high cheek bones, their automatic weapons slung across their chests or at the ready. She thought it probable that bandits still roamed parts of the countryside, and that harems continued clandestinely to exist—though she found comfort in supposing herself too old a candidate for one. Others of her sex, less cautious by nature than she, would surely think twice about traveling by themselves here, or staying overnight alone. Certainly her best friend Judy, her sister-in-law Marina, or any number of her acquaintances at Fitness Plus, would have had qualms about the prospect. And with the unpleasant and unaccountable Mr Malcolm (now to be so designated, she decided) thrown into the bargain, surely not one of them would have dreamt of it! Pictures formed: Judy's, then Marina's, reaction on finding herself left alone in the middle of Turkey with Mr Malcolm there to add insult to injury. Marina would have spent the night phoning embassies, taxis, Kadir; Judy would have piled furniture against the door, popped a couple of Valiums, gone to bed in her coat—zipped up to the neck!

She had wanted to visit Greece, not Turkey at all; but Mario had found no other tour in March. 'And you had to have it early, didn't you; so you could be back in time to greet the swallows and to see all your spring flowers sprouting.' He had assured her that Turkey was perfectly safe, especially now the military had taken control; and that when the tour went on to Greece she would have ample time to see all the Byzantine churches she wanted. 'The last time you went there was some trouble,' she'd ventured to remind him. 'Darling, do you think I'd send you there if I weren't sure it was a safe country?' he had responded, in the rich, even-flowing voice she had once admired and still thought of as having the colour of molten gold. 'You'll be in a bus the whole time. You'll be with thirty other people—people from home!'

She could scarcely accuse her husband of indifference, because he had much on his mind these days; yet surprisingly she found herself for an instant vindictively questioning his genuinely caring which country or countries she visited; wondering if he might not have offered, in the circumstances, glib comfort had the plan for her been to bicycle through Tibet or paddle up the Blue Nile, so long as she got out of his hair for a time, left him to make the deals which meant so much to him. An aberrant thought. She was doing him an injustice. A monstrous injustice. But *safe on a bus with people from home*!—her husband's confident assertion was ironically wide of the mark. She half wished him here now, at the bus stop—long enough, at least, for her to tell him so.

But her being left behind by the tour bus wasn't Mario's fault; she could not blame him for this, any more than for anything else.

She thought again of their parting at JFK. Scurrying beyond the swing doors of the section designated 'Passengers Only,' aware that he could no longer follow, she had felt butterflies of panic at being separated from him, an awareness of undefined perils awaiting her; but at the same time of welcome possibilities, vital opportunities—before the flight announcement had returned her to the exigencies of the moment. What were those possibilities? And those opportunities—to do what, exactly?

Now, with her back to the chill spring wind sweeping in from the not far distant sea she stared along the road that led through the town. The shops and low apartment buildings struck her as nondescript, devoid of promise of any kind, looking as though they had been erected hastily and without much thought after an earthquake. She could see into an open-fronted restaurant or *café* that was crowded with black-clad men who gave the impression that they had all murdered their wives and were relaxing after a mass funeral. In the opposite direction, the direction of Izmir, the road stretched featureless, dust-coloured, empty, to the low hills; looking like a road in a western.

I needn't stay, she told herself. Really I needn't. The bus will be coming any minute now.

She saw herself securely installed on the bus heading back to Izmir. A two-hour journey at most. It would be full of local farmers, possibly animals. A *dolmush*, Trevor Malcolm had called it. But even if it smelt she would be left to herself, an object of mild curiosity but surely not of hostility. At the other end there would be a taxi to whisk her from the bus depot to the steps of the hotel. She imagined kicking off her shoes in the room she shared with Gloria Bloomquist at the Izmir Palas, watching the sun going down into the Aegean, pampering herself primping in the gaily tiled modern bathroom. And next day she would head out with the tour again. With people from home.

Here the sun, which had been more in than out in the last few minutes, went in once more and the world turned abruptly darker. Sparse, heavy, raindrops struck the road surface like stray bullets and made the dust spurt up. The man in front of Carey Signorello lifted an empty willow basket to protect his bald head. Another in a torn parka flicked away his cigarette and coughed. His baloon-trousered wife shifted their string-trussed bag closer to the curb, claiming territory. Minutes passed and the raindrops slackened. There came a stirring and all at once a collective murmur of approval as the bus came in sight.

Seconds before it drew up, Carey Signorello broke from the queue and crossed the road—in contradiction to her fears, to her own nature as she had come to view it, and to the recent omen of the raindrops.

A man in a black knitted sailor's toque, who was tending a fruit and vegetable stand, the blue and yellow awnings of which hung between the road and the front door of the Hotel Croesus, paused with an orange in each hand to admire the young woman as she passed. He shook his head, grinned to himself, while gently balancing the oranges in his palms. Deeming that he saw through her assumed briskness, he clicked his tongue. He sympathized with the sudden hesitancy now overtaking her. Seeing her standing alone, suitcase-less and irresolute before the open door of the hotel, he sent the scarlet tip of his tongue over his lower lip. If only she could have come over a little more his way, under one of his awnings. In fancy he addressed her boldly, yet gently and of course politely.—I have a dwelling, snug with hangings, carpeted, close by, very close—he imagined himself saying. It would cost you nothing; as my guest I would not charge you a single lira. In your sweet company I would not dream of such a thing, not I! Nor would I misbehave, for I am no longer young; and besides, we men of Anatolia are men of honour.

Still, it would not do. He knew perfectly well. The forwardness would not. An invitation to a cup of *çai*, yes—that would have been in order, and quite enough, had she come closer to the awning.

But she had not; and now he saw her enter the hotel.

He set to thinking: How can they be left like this, quite alone and unprotected, such women? Are they not like flowers woven into a silk hanging, or flowers to be admired in a garden, flowers that are to be fenced off from harm and kept so they be not trodden upon and spoiled? Recalling something in her expression, something at odds with timidity—*hunger*, of a kind, perhaps—he frowned.

Turning away, he dismissed the thought—as, gently, he replaced the oranges, cradling them in a newspaper-lined tray.

## Chapter 3

SHIELDING HER FACE with her free hand she edged through the beaded curtain that swung across the doorway of the hotel and paused to allow her eyes to adjust to the gloom. The marble interior of the lobby exuded an unwelcoming chill, and her heart sank before the Spartan drabness of the place; though not squalor it was like nothing she was used to. Reaching the desk she made out against one wall a heavily built man dozing in an armchair with his face hidden under a multi-coloured newspaper, and beside him a cage containing two canaries. A notion seized her that she did not belong. There could be no retreat, however: her fingers had already touched the small brass bell on the desk. The man grunted and swept the newspaper to the floor. Two smudgy black lines, of moustache and hooked-together eyebrows, bobbed up in the gloom like globules of crude oil. From their cage the birds twittered excitement as their keeper struggled to his feet from the low and evidently broken-springed armchair and hastened to meet the foreigner.

Mr Deverli, manager of the Hotel Croesus, prided himself on speaking not just German, as did a number of his countrymen owing to the caprices of history, but English too. Carey Signorello's obvious relief at this pleased him instantly. Introducing himself, he saw that she was attractive and alone, and, like the fruit vendor under the blue and yellow awnings in the square outside, he heaved a mental sigh in acknowledgement of her person and circumstances. How well formed these American women are! he thought. Up to a certain age. Daily exercise and a scientifically balanced diet. Still, he would not want his own wife bothering about such things; he was content to have her let herself go, sparing him much expense and possibly worry. He nodded vigorous but decorous encouragement as the newcomer recounted recent events with a slightly quivering smile, and stated nervously and at charming but unnecessary length her altogether obvious requirements.

Mr Deverlli made his large chunky face assume what he

deemed an appropriately pained expression, but it was not long before he was licking the ends of his fierce moustache involuntarily and waggling his stubbled dewlaps in genuine perplexity. Incredible, that such a thing should happen! He expressed shock, sorrow, profound regret, that the lady should have suffered this indignity in his country; that she should have been left behind by a tour bus! How, he wondered, could the organizers of the tour have been so negligent? Never had he heard of such a thing. It was an outrage, and certainly the Central Tourist Office and the Tourist Police must be informed. He himself would undertake to do so if the lady would permit him. Every tourist was a guest—a *misafir*—in Turkey, and was to be treated courteously at all times according to age-old Anatolian rules of hospitality. Besides, the tourist industry was vital to the economy—the country just getting on its feet again after the recent troubles with Communist agitators and terrorists of various stripe, and then the military take-over, and now this talk of war with Greece—

'War—!'

'Talk,' Mr Deverli quickly added. 'No truth to it. Always there is enmity, but not war, not real war. Talk, only talk, Mrs Signorello.' But that she should be left without a suitcase! he hurried on. So inconvenient! He slapped his glistening dome-shaped head with a huge hand, on the fingers of which lay ringlets of thick black hair. Perhaps she would like to borrow a nightdress from his wife, who was larger than she—but still, for one night—? If the lady would condescend to borrow it he would deliver it himself. (Indeed, he would even take the precaution, he instantly resolved, of fetching it now, as his wife was away and he had an assignation with another woman who might not receive his explanation kindly.)

The effort required of Carey to pacify the excitable hotelier, to dissuade him from informing the tourist authorities or the police, and to convince him that she could manage for one night without his borrowing for her a nightdress from his wife, had a beneficial effect on her. She acknowledged his concern to be not entirely theatrical and was grateful for that portion of it that was genuine. She began to feel less desolate, less apprehensive about her surroundings, more confident that in staying over in Selçuk she had done the right thing. Surely she could survive without luxury for one night, for the sake of a novel and perhaps enlightening experience; and for the beneficial effect it might have on her? With Mr Deverli's help she telephoned the Izmir Palas, and when informed that the tour bus had not yet returned with Kadir, the guide, she left a message saying she would return by local bus to Izmir the following evening in time to rejoin the tour for its journey on to Troy, Boursa and Istanbul the next day.

'All our rooms have showers,' Mr Deverli announced proudly, when she returned his ballpoint after writing in the register. 'But should you desire hot water it will be necessary to inform me or one of my staff a half hour in advance.'

Staff?—There seemed to be no one of the kind in the whole echo-prone building. 'Yes, I think I'd like some,' she said smiling.

The brows lowered momentarily. 'It is the wood—'

'The wood,' she repeated, at a loss.

'I will see to it so soon as you are settled in a room. And a cup of tea, of *çai*, yes?—While waiting.' He stumped to the doorway and parted the beaded curtain; she heard him instantly call, apparently without having ascertained the presence of anyone in particular, '*Cai! Cai, istiyorum*!'

Glancing over the long wooden board on which room keys dangled above the counter she noted some twenty numbers and keys for all except one, Room 7.

Her host returned, snatched several keys from the board and started for the stairs. 'Be so kind as to come with me,' he said, smiling happily. 'The season is young and you may choose the room you like best. But be careful, for the stairs are wet.'

Wet indeed. Little waterfalls ran down them. Carey found the upper floor awash.

'Rain this morning,' her escort explained. 'It will go away. It will pass. Take no notice.'

'Your hotel is almost empty,' she remarked.

'The season is young,' he repeated.

'You have one other guest, however—?'

'One other, yes.'

'Is he—?'

'Quiet, very quiet. He will not bother you.' He opened a door, only to close if hastily. 'Wet, a little.'

She hung back while he leant into another room, then another. The problem was not one of choosing the most pleasant room but of discovering a room that did not have a quarter of an inch of rain water slicking its bare marble floor. Being fatigued and still nervous at the novelty of her undertaking she felt the onset of something like an attack of schoolgirlish giggles and wondered in alarm how long she could hold out.

'Ah!'—Flinging wide the shutters of another room for her inspection—'This one is dry, you see!'

A square wooden table, an upright chair, a bed with a stringy green spread, a spindly-legged bedside table bearing a shadeless lamp, and a chipped ashtray, presented themselves as her host stepped back triumphantly from the window frame. Adjoining was a small mould-scented bathroom with basin, toilet and shower.

'Good,' she said, feigning an enthusiasm she was far from feeling. 'I'll take it.'

Mr Deverli expressed satisfaction at the wisdom of her decision and departed, to reappear moments later with a boy carrying a tray on which was set a small glass cup of clear brown liquid. 'Your *çai*, Madam,' Removing the cup officiously and slopping it slightly, he placed it on the table.

'Shall I—?' she began, touching her shoulder bag. But he was already letting himself out, shooing the boy before him.

Cradling the glass cup in her hand, Carey glanced about the room, a room unlike any room she had slept in. The novelty of its plainness, of its ugliness, shocked and amused her. An uncluttered room, a no-frills room, but one in which nothing could hide or disguise itself at least. She finished the *çai* and set down the cup, feeling suddenly exhausted, yet elated at what she had done. Not long ago her friend Marina had accused her, only half jokingly, of never taking any serious step without waiting for one of her 'signs.' On this occasion the unpredictability, the implicit spontaneity, the audacity, were to be wondered at.

A smell reached her, languorous and sweet, like marijuana. It flashed on her mind that Mr Deverli had slipped something into her *çai;* but then she thought of the military crack-down, the harsh penalties she'd read about. Perhaps the smell came from the room of Trevor Malcolm? She caught another whiff—and laughed at herself. 'It's wood! Some sort of wood—being burned to heat the water for my shower!'

She had not asked about dinner, assuming from what she'd been used to that the hotel would have a restaurant. Recollecting a sign of some sort in the corridor, she opened the door a crack and saw curiously written: *This way to Hell of Brakfast*, with a drooping cardboard arrow pointing to the stairs. It didn't matter, she told herself, quietly closing and locking the door. After the shower she would lie down and quickly fall asleep. Venturing out alone in Selçuk was unthinkable. She pictured herself in the restaurant she'd noticed earlier, crowded with funereal figures, all male. No, she'd do without dinner, get a good sleep and then after breakfast tomorrow go straight off to see Ephesus properly. She'd do the ruins justice, in defiance of the tour and Trevor Malcolm.

Her thoughts were disrupted as sunlight flooded the room, altering the look of things: the wall above the bed's head had suffered an attack of measles—bumps with attendant shadows sprang from it here and there. Kicking off her shoes she stood on the bed to examine them: the remains of blood-laden mosquitoes from last year or the year before, squashed and left glued like trophies! A shadow startled her by landing on the wallpaper: a stork was teetering on a large ramshakle nest built outside her window in the aqueduct. The bird seemed to try a slow wink at her, raising and lowering a shutter-like eyelid, then stretching its neck away towards the sky and working its scruffy body gingerly down in the nest. She stole to the window and watched it seeming to enjoy the meagre warmth of the now mostly shrouded sun.

By leaning out she could see a medieval castle on a rise of ground, white-washed houses with terra cotta roofs, orange groves and fields of artichokes. A mist rose from the ground and threaded the trees. Castle and houses, roads and fields, stones and trees, appeared as kindred shapes, their outlines dissolved in washes of pale gold and grey. On the roof of the apartment building next to the hotel, a line of white and black clothes twitched fitfully against the patchy blue and gunmetal sky. Beneath the hotel sign in the square the fruit and vegetable man, having stored his produce, was hauling down the metal shutter, securing it, slouching off.

Carey's gaze, resting now on the hotel sign, brought the word *Croesus* to mind; though she could not see the lettering. How odd to be here, she thought; because people sometimes said of Mario—jokingly, of course, but really meaning it—that he was 'rich as Croesus.'

Turning inside, she reflected that had she been next to Trevor Malcolm's room or even near it she would have heard something, notwithstanding what Mr Deverli had said. Bare marble and concrete, suited to the long hot summers. They were the hotel's only occupants, he and she. The thought stirred her strangely.

From time to time she entered the small windowless bathroom to try the hot water tap of the shower and when at last warm water flowed from it she undressed, spread her clothes neatly on the bed and returned with a small bar of soap—courtesy British Airways—from her bag. The water flowed into a drain hole in the middle of the bathroom floor. There was no shower curtain, no enclosure. She felt her nakedness, and curiously exposed. Soaping her legs she thought how shaky they'd felt in the parking lot at Ephesus.

She dried herself and searched her face in the mirror. The bulb over the basin couldn't have been more than a twenty. It set large grey circles under her eyes and lent a greenish tinge to her wheaten hair. She was glad she'd had the hair cut shorter for the trip. That too seemed to promise a change. She twisted a hand towel round her head in a turban and slipped into her raincoat, shivering with the chill of the material against her skin; then went and turned down the bed and lay on her back gazing at the slain mosquitoes on the walls and ceiling. She tried to relax, taking several deep breaths, slowly exhaling each time. She made fists, released them; waggled her toes, drew circles in the air with them.

I should be able to sleep now, after the *çai* and the shower, she told herself. Soon it will be dark.

She undid the belt of the raincoat and let the folds fall on either side of her body. Gripping the cool brass of the bedstead above her head, as though her wrists were tied there, and wriggling the rest of her down to her full extent, she closed her eyes and saw him—walking slightly in front against the trees and fields and sky. Undeniably good-looking, in a rough-edged, craggy, sort of way. Irresistible to women who liked that sort of thing, no doubt; but certainly not to her. Without much class, judging by the scruffy jacket and baggy jeans. She heard the gruff voice—the accent not English but Scottish, now she recalled it—coming from a clenched mouth that seemed to grudge being opened a smidgeon more than necessary. The grey eyes charged with unaccountable anger. And his age?—forty-five, maybe. Unfair: more like thirty-eight or forty. Hair greying at the temples—a feature not to be interpreted as attractive outside a romantic novel. 'Romantic' was right, though, she conceded; he made you feel there was some secret connected with him.

She shivered anew, turned on her side, closed and tucked up her legs so the raincoat covered them. All was as quiet as before, except that her tummy rumbled. Without something to eat she might not get to sleep, tired though she was: Why not ask Mr Deverli for a yogurt and maybe some crackers? The idea, coming quite naturally, agitated her oddly; and seeing herself venturing beyond the locked door, she felt her heartbeat accelerate. No, she told herself; forget it. I'll do something else entirely, wash a couple of things. With luck they'll be dry by tomorrow. She dressed at once, entered the bathroom, saw her pale grey face resurface in the mirror.

There was no plug for the basin.—How do they expect you to wash, soak anything, if there's no plug?—She hesitated before the mirror, smoothed a hank of hair at her temple, then turned – suddenly resolved to ask Mr Deverli for a plug, along with a yogurt and some crackers. Elated, nervous, she unlocked the door, opened it an inch or so, listened; then let herself out and proceeded warily for the stairs, reading beneath her breath the numbers on the doors as they drew level with her eye, and concluding that Room 7 lay down the hall the other way.

Gaining the stairs she heard the sound of snoring.

She hesitated, cautiously descended, until half way down she caught sight of Mr Deverli, stretched out in the deep, broken-springed chair. Pages of the multi-coloured newspaper lay to left and right of him. A badly stained canvas cover had been thrown over the birdcage. Quietly, her heart beating strangely faster, she retreated to the top of the stairs and stood irresolute.

A minute later she saw as from a distance herself walking back along the corridor, passing the door to her own room, halting before another's.

## Chapter 4

He was lying on the narrow saggy bed fully dressed when the knock came, followed at once by Carey's 'Mr Malcolm, are you there?'

He shot up, swearing beneath his breath at the pain in his neck and shoulder which the sudden movement caused him. At the door, he did not at first understand what she was trying to tell him.

'A plug.' She stood well back in the corridor.

'A *what*?'

'Yes, I've come to borrow a plug.' Her voice shook slightly.

'A plug?'

'Yes—you know, for the basin. My basin hasn't got one.'

'No one's has,' he responded at last, momentarily convulsed by silent laughter. 'Come in.'

Struck by the boldness and absurdity of what she was doing, Carey coloured deeply. She told herself that however original and commendable her decision to stay over, this secondary decision was a bad one. To have knocked on this man's door for this ludicrous reason! What had possessed her to do such a fool thing?

'Come in,' he repeated, turning away. 'Didn't happen to see someone else out there?'

'Someone else?—No.'

'Well, that's good. Just ourselves, then.' He had kept watch at the window, seen no yellow Mercedes, and begun to think himself unsuspected and unsought by the man he had passed on the path.

So he'd been expecting someone, Carey thought. A woman?—'What do you mean, "No one's has?"' He had gone into the bathroom and didn't answer. His room was a Spartan as hers and furnished identically except it was untidy—remarkably so, considering the few resources apparently available to make it so. Assigned to the floor were several paperbacks and a toppled pile of papers, a backpack, a tumbler and wine bottle. The pale green bedspread was rumpled. She recognised the Marks & Spencer shopping bag he'd had on the walk from Ephesus; it hung from the one straight-backed chair. 'I went down to Mr Deverli,' she heard herself call after him. 'He was asleep.'

He reappeared, disconcertingly jaunty now, tossing a small black object in front of him and clawing it out of the air as he neared her. She tried to guess what he would do.—How dangerous was he? I should never have knocked, she told herself. He's been drinking. I don't believe this is happening.

'My very own plug, this.' He halted in front of her. 'Brought if from Dundee. Canny, eh? In Turkey they assume you'll bring one with you, except in the posh hotels. People used to walk off with them, so they became rare, you see; then non-existent.'

'Ah—'

'And it has a certain sentimental value, this wee plug. I don't know I should be entrusting it to a stranger.' He whipped the hand holding the plug behind his back. 'Come in,' he said once more. 'Missed the *dolmush*, did you? I'll no bite you, and you can try a drop of Turkish wine.—You'll not have had that on your tour.'

The invitation was surely not what she expected—or wanted? She was trembling.

He smiled broadly. 'Aye, and a bite to eat as well. Humble repast, nothing fancy mind. Some confabulation, too. You never know, we might get on, find we have something in common.' He laughed and shook his head.

Carey's heart-beat accelerated. Scenting danger, she was drawn to it; as she had been drawn to enter the Hotel Croesus rather than take the *dolmush* back to Izmir. It was all quite strange.

'Well?'

'I—'

'No drinkee, no plugee,' he quipped. 'Think about it.' With which he tossed the small black plug in the air and managed to catch it inches from her nose. His sleeve was rolled up—the arm, bare from the biceps, tanned, muscular.

'At the parking lot in Ephesus—,' she began accusingly.

'Oh aye, the parking lot.'

'Yes, at the parking lot when we met, and on our walk, you were—'

'*Un peu distrait*?'

'Not nice. Not helpful. Deliberately—'

'Dammit, I got you to the bus, or at least to the bus stop.' He scratched his head. 'But you're here and not on your way back to Izmir. So what happened? You're good at missing buses, I must say.'

'Reluctantly, you got me there. I had to beg. In the parking lot you refused to listen.' It was much the best thing, safer, to go on accusing him; she managed to sound quite angry.

'He gave a tight-lipped smile, and shook his head. 'Well, one is not always—'

'I don't care if you were preoccupied about something. I was in a real jam.'

'Ay, that's it. I was preoccupied. *Le mot juste.*—Look, lassie, for godsake don't hang about in the corridor! Come in, come in!' He stepped briskly aside for her to enter.

She found herself doing so—feeling a vague and oddly detached concern, broken by a little leap of heart on hearing the door at her back being closed and locked. Concern, and at the same time something that was not concern, something that made her wonder at herself. It was as though all this were happening to someone else, and she did not mind now so much as she would have before.

'For you,' he said, bowing stiffly and presenting her with the plug. 'A *memento bagnio*. Please, do sit ... there.' He swept to the floor the contents of the room's one chair and bowed to her.

Conscious of the bed opposite, she sat primly, crossed her legs and arms, watched in silence as he turned his attention to the table: snatching from it a writing pad and envelopes, repositioning it so as to make it reachable from chair and bed, placing upon it in quick succession three small brown paper bags, a couple of plastic plates, a tumbler, and a wine bottle which was not the one from the floor.

The bed bothered her. She would like to have risen, while his back was turned, to smooth the pale green bedspread, tuck it in a neat line under the pillow.

'I was wanting to visit the castle,' he said off-handedly. 'Selçuk Castle, you know? You can see it from the window. And the Temple of Artemis, just beside it.'

She watched him approach the window and look quickly—not towards the castle, however, but directly down into the street.

'Meant to go this afternoon, on the way back from Ephesus; but with one thing and another—'

She saw him draw a red Swiss army knife from his pocket and with its corkscrew begin opening the wine: gripping the bottle between his knees—thrusting, twisting, tugging, conveying to her an impression of vigour and overkill that she found disconcerting. 'Don't go to any trouble; I won't stay long.'

'As I say, the Temple of Artemis is there, too, beside the castle. Reduced to a single column, now though. Artemis the great mother, the many-breasted—you know the statue? But the breasts aren't breasts, they're bull's testicles. Power, potency, virility—'

He was frowning darkly, almost comically, concentrating now on probing with his little finger in the neck of the bottle for a piece of cork. At length he asked, more as though he were considering, and to himself rather than to her: 'How the bejesus can anyone get left behind by a tour bus?'

He had asked before, during their walk. She felt it tiresome of him to ask again. 'I told you, I don't know. I haven't a clue.'

Her attention was drawn to steps some distance down the hall. Trevor Malcolm was listening too. His visitor? .... A woman's steps. Another's joined them. Then came a male voice, the voice of Mr Deverli. It had been left to someone else to waken him. Steps and voices faded.

'There's dried apricots,' he said, gazing on the small crammed table with apparent satisfaction. 'And nuts—hazel nuts, not pistachios (they're imported)—and feta cheese—you like feta chees? Some people can't stand it because it's goaty. Well, it's from goats, after all; and biscuits (crackers, to you), and some *ekmek*, and wine too, of course—Doluca, good Turkish wine—to go with it. Have you had any dinner?'

'No,' she grudgingly admitted, now thoroughly cross at herself for being hungry and at him for being hectic. 'What's *ekmek*?'

'You haven't had dinner? Good, good—'

'*Ekmek*—?' she persisted.

'Bread. *Ekmek*'s bread. Staff of life. Well, the other staff of life,' he added crudely, but the remark passed her by.

'Ah.'

The act of retrieving the second tumbler from the floor brought him a spasm of pain, which produced an audible gasp.

'You've hurt you neck,' she remarked, deriving some small satisfaction from the fact.

'I wanted to see into that castle before dark,' he said again, ignoring this. 'And go over the Artemis site. Felt a bit restless. Have you been?—No, of course not. The tour ... I mean, on a tour you're always—'

To this desultory talk of his she attached a picture of the castle she had seen from her window, listened at the same time for more footsteps in the corridor, wondered who it was he might know in Selçuk.

'Fruit and nuts and wine,' he said. 'Classical fare. The staples of the ancients. Nourishing. You get used to keeping a supply on hand when you're travelling in this country. That way you're never stuck. I don't bother with restaurants much, travelling alone. Eat in my room, go to bed early, virtuous life.' He dumped the contents of a paper bag onto a plastic plate.

Together they picked at the nuts and apricots, the cheese, the *ekmek*, sluicing them down with mouthfulls of the dark red wine, while shadows took possession of the far corners of the room—and Carey remained alert for the steps of the visitor Trevor Malcolm had surely been expecting.

'So you decided to stay over and see Ephesus properly tomorrow morning?' He looked full at her for the first time.

'I had no idea it was like that.'

'How so?'

'I came on this trip looking forward more to the Byzantine, the Christian, stuff than to the Graeco-Roman; with Ephesus it was the house of the Virgin Mary I wanted to see, and the place where Paul preached. But the whole feeling, the atmosphere, is so powerfully—'

'Pagan.'

'Yes.'

'Ephesus still belongs to Artemis; her shrines, arches, and fountains; her paved streets and market places; her broken statuary, baths and library; her brothel.'

'Brothel?' She had still to see it.

'Yes. Rationally placed, next to the library.—You disapprove of that?'

She flushed. 'Of course I do.'

'What, the brothel; or it's being rationally placed next to the library?—You'll see it tomorrow; but don't bother with the house of the Virgin because it's bogus.'

He was laughing at her now, thinking what a prude, what a New England Puritan, she was. She said nothing and sat up straighter in the flimsy upright chair. Had there really been a brothel, or was he making it up? Naked bodies lolling back on the sun-warmed stones, welcoming toga-ed customers with open legs. 'I walked all the way along the street of the Merchants,' she said quickly. 'And the Arcadian Way before that, of course.'

He cleared his throat, nodded vigorously, then winced with pain. 'Mmmm, it's a great place. Gives you a feeling, as you say. Do you know, when Byron visited it there was almost nothing? Buried. He sat there musing and wondering but all the time it was right there under his backside!'

How different Trevor Malcolm was from people on the tour! Alarmed at being momentarily caught up in his sudden burst of enthusiasm she volunteered only the briefest of smiles.

'Yes, Ephesus is quite something,' he hurried on. 'But one day Aphrodisias will be comparable, maybe better.'

'Aphrodisias?'

'Mmm, at Karakasu, inland from here, not far. A Graeco-Roman city dedicated to Venus, or Aphrodite. Unbelievable. It's only now being dug up—by yours truly, among others. Trouble is, we're out of money.'

So Trevor Malcolm was an archaeologist! She found herself confiding to him that once upon a time she had wanted to be exactly that. 'Yes, I liked the idea of digging up bits of pottery and so on, and piecing them together until they made sense,' she concluded.

'You got married instead.' He poured them both more wine. 'A mistake, was it? To get married instead of piecing things together until they made sense?'

She bridled. 'Not at all.'

'So what do you find to do, married, back in Massachusetts?'

'New Jersey.' She gave him a look, before deciding to answer. 'I garden, among other things. I adore my garden.'

'Ah, you do that sort of digging. Weeds, daffodil bulbs, and so on.'

'Exactly,' she smilingly responded, seeing herself in her straw hat telling William, the old gardener who'd been there forever, which bulbs were to go where.

'Well, I was married to someone who also liked digging. She was a vicious little *gold*-digger, name of Suzanne. I say "gold-digger", but of course I had no gold. It was funny as hell. And not so funny. In fact it's the sort of thing to make a man cynical about the sex.' He shot her a glance, grimaced. 'She'd read an article on a find I'd made, of a few Ottoman coins and stuff; an article that puffed the thing up as a major discovery of Turkish treasures, and gave the impression they were mine to keep, instead of the Turkish government's.'

He shook his head. 'You think you know a person, understand them—only to realise you've made them up and they're something else altogether.'

'Oh, I understand my husband, Mario,' she said with a laugh. 'After seven years of marriage.'

'Doesn't mean a thing. It's hard enough getting to know yourself.—What's he do?'

'He deals in *objets d'art*—antique jewellery, icons, things for private collectors and museums.'

'Mmm, dangerous.'

'Dangerous?'

'Aye, if you forget to sign the right papers, or sign the wrong ones, then try taking stuff like that out of the country, you can find yourself in prison. There are types in sites like Ephesus and Pergamum and Didyma who'll open their coats and flash a terra cotta head or a marble figurine and then when you've bought it go and get paid again by some bloke in the Police or Customs, who'll arrest you. Nowadays the national heritage is taken pretty seriously.'

'My husband was always aware of the rules and respected them, I'm sure. He's sold to the Metropolitan.' His comment brought her sharply to Mario's defence.

'Of course.'

'He's ... a few years older than me,' she added, without knowing why.

'And kids?'

'Oh, children. No, I couldn't—'

Trevor Malcolm briskly explained that he'd come to Turkey as part of an international team under a Dr Edrin of the University of Istanbul to work on the Aphrodisias site. 'I've taken this week off to touch base with the University, try to scrape up some more funds so we can continue, and also compare a couple of things with Ephesus.'

'Try to scrape up more funds?—You mean you really might have to stop, with Aphrodisias? Because of money?'

'Because of the lack of it. Might have to, yes. It's looking more and more that way.' He poured himself more wine.

'There's another bottle, an open one, over there on the floor.' She knew the comment to be a criticism; she had been on the lookout for an opportunity to make it.

'So there is!' he laughed. 'I expect you've phoned, about that silly bus?'

'To the hotel in Izmir, yes.'

'And?'

'And nothing. They weren't back yet. I had to leave a message.'

He sighed and shook his head. Aegean Sun-Fun Tours. The idea of grown-up people allowing themselves to be herded like sheep, sticking with their own kind, staying at their own sort of hotels, with bacon and eggs and ketchup and hamburgers in plentiful supply.

'Mr Malcolm,' she began, partly reading his thoughts and feeling a need to put him right.

'Call me Trevor.'

'Trevor, then—'

'You see how nice I'm being to you now? I could've said call me *Dr.* Malcolm.'

'Trevor. As a matter of fact,' she earnestly persisted, raising her eyes to his, 'I don't enjoy travelling with a lot of other people on a bus. I'm really a loner. And I hate being rushed. I seem to take longer than anybody else. In Ephesus the only thing I wanted was to get away from the person who'd been talking non-stop to me on the bus, to get away by myself and see the things I'd started reading about in my guide book. It was really great to be alone, and it was such a surprise, Ephesus. But I couldn't have come to Turkey on my own, after all.'

'Why didn't your husband come and take you around?'

'He can't just drop his business. He arranged the tour, did all the planning.'

'Doesn't travel, like certain wines?'

'He does travel, quite a lot in fact, on business. He's been here to Turkey several times.'

He eased his legs onto the bed and propped himself against its single pillow. 'So that's why you got left behind. Didn't stick with the flock.'

She frowned and shook her head. 'No, because I told the guide what I was doing and I made sure he understood. I'm cautious by nature.'

'Cautious, eh? I'm the opposite. I'm not at all cautious. I leap, then look.' Despite having just settled himself, he rose, emptied some remnants of food into one of the brown paper bags, and—apparently having no immediate intention to tidy up further—went again to look from the window into the street.

'You can get into trouble that way,' she said, raising her voice above the horn of a passing car that was playing *La Cucheracha.*

'I have. I *do*.' He turned stiffly from the window with an impatient grunt.

There followed a pause, which she felt to weigh on them but which he seemed disinclined to break. She saw herself waiting in the road for the bus, the rain beginning, staring across at the hotel sign, trying to decide. 'And Croesus?' she ventured, thinking at length that she must say something. 'The name of the hotel … I've forgotten who he was.'

He looked inquiringly at her, seeming not to have heard.

'Croesus?'

'Oh, Croesus. He was the last king of Lydia, this region.'

'A king. And very rich.'

'The richest man in the ancient world.'

'Proverbial—'

'Yes. "As rich as Croesus."'

'He didn't … swallow his children, too?' She shuddered at the thought.

'That was Cronos.'

'Ah—'

'I don't remember what happened to Croesus's children.'

'Lived happily ever after, I guess. With all that money.'

'The root of all evil—and happily ever after? You think so? Well maybe the children did, but that wasn't how things turned out for the old man himself.'

She waited. He poured himself another tumbler of Doluca, settled himself again on the bed; then related how, in fulfillment of a prophecy, or curse, consequent on a crime of an ancestor, one Gyges, Croesus had lost his immense riches, his vast empire, and died a prisoner of his enemy, the Persian king, Cyrus the Great.

'And Gyges's crime? What was it?'

He frowned. All he could remember was that Gyges had murdered a king and taken his queen and his kingdom, and the Oracle of Delphi had pronounced a doom on Gyges's descendant of the fifth generation, who happened to be Croesus.

The story affected her strangely; she darted him a look that seemed accusatory. It was a wild exaggeration to call Mario, her husband, 'rich as Croesus,' as people did; but he was undeniably rich, even now when things weren't going so well for him as they had before; and in a small village in Calabria, before coming to the United States, his father had stabbed his best friend and married his beautiful widow. It was silly of course, the connection; and Mario did not, after all, represent the fifth generation. Still, she silently prayed that Mario, so deservedly prosperous, so blessed as he was, would not lose everything, and die like Croesus.

She rose abruptly. 'May I go rinse my sticky fingers?—Then I must go get some sleep.'

'Be my guest. But is something wrong? Something I said?'

'No nothing.—The wine, maybe. I'm tired and shouldn't have had a second glass.' But it was not the wine. It was the story, the myth or history of Croesus and his ancestor, Gyges; and the fleeting, quite outlandish notion, that—obscurely—this man, Trevor Malcolm, represented a threat to her husband, to Mario.

In the bathroom hung an imperfectly washed tee-shirt in which pale red stains still showed. On the floor next to the drain hole for the shower a sketchbook, its pages marred by stains of similar but deeper hue, had been propped, spine uppermost, to dry. A shiver ran through her. She stooped, took up the sketchbook and gingerly turned the partially stuck-together pages: drawings of temples and statuary, an annotated plan of a section of Ephesus, another marked 'Aphrodisias—Agora.' Whatever had made the stains had rippled the edges of the pages and spoiled some of their content. Were they from wine, the stains—*or blood*?

Disconcerted, anxious for enlightenment but afraid to seek it, she re-entered the bedroom. Her host stood with his back to the window and the last light, his features undistinguishable. The long shadow of his stiff upper body leapt out across the marble as though to entwine itself about her ankles. She opened her mouth to speak, merely to repeat her intention of leaving, of returning to her room for the night, but she was at once struck by his form—darkly silhouetted, seeming abruptly larger, filling the window frame, and as though poised to swoop down to attack or embrace her.

The next moment a sound broke in, a strange sound, which, before she could place it, caused in her a vivid rippling, a vibration of mind and body. Upon her it broke with an almost physical violence. It was a sound invading and filing her whole being with a sense of the sadness, and menace, of the ages. She had never heard it in her life before or anything quite like it, yet it came as something familiar, timeless, unsettling. From a nearby minaret the *muezzin* was summoning the faithful to prayer. The voice, electronically amplified, came as a protracted groan, then a cry that pierced the hearer and had in it pain and passionate yearning. It swelled, changed pitch, an incantation at once dissonant, ugly (melodic and beautiful also, perhaps, though Carey was not just then receptive to any such positive qualities). It rose and fell, trailed off to a sigh, surged anew. She listened intently until it ceased—to be replaced by the barking of several dogs.

A low chuckle broke from the dark figure against the window. 'I've noticed that. The dogs. Afterwards they howl. Either that hurts their eardrums or they're worried Allah won't make room for them in heaven.'

'What was it saying?'

'"*Allah ekbar, Allah ekbar*—Allah is great, there is no god but he, and Mohammud is his prophet"—something like that, and more of the same.'

'It has a beauty, I'm sure,' she said with a shiver. 'Yet it was eerie. It made me feel—' But she could not describe quite what it made her feel.

'That you are in Turkey?' he offered, mocking now. 'And you'd rather be in Thessaloniki, listening to the chants of the bearded priests of Orthodoxy.'

'That's on the tour, too,' she said affecting a laugh. 'Next week. But I did like Ephesus. And I'm looking forward to going back there tomorrow morning and seeing what I didn't have time for today.'

'I've had enough of Ephesus,' he said. 'I'm never going back.'

'Never?' It came as a surprise, after she'd heard him enthuse about the place.

'I've developed an aversion to it. Something unpleasant happened to me there, that's all.'

'And what was that?'

He did not reply. And, set against the last light, the features of his face gave nothing away. She thanked him, turned to go. He remained motionless. They parted—she smitten anew and powerfully with the conviction that he was alien, inscrutable, probably dangerous, and best left alone. She thanked him again for the plug and said she would leave it for him with Mr Deverli at the desk, should they fail to meet at breakfast.

'Fail to meet—' He spoke, but merely to echo her, as she unlocked the door and let herself thankfully out.

## Chapter 5

SHE WOKE AT dawn with a dream unfinished. Gloria Bloomquist had urged her to have an affair—and with a man called Gyges. Gloria, who scarcely knew her. She felt indignant at Gloria for suggesting such a thing, even in a dream.

When unfamiliar birds' songs yielded to traffic and snatches of foreign conversation from passers-by she lay staring at the slain mosquitoes on the ceiling and thinking what else had occurred during the paper bag picnic of the night before. Now, in the pale light of a new day, she reminded herself that she had decided definitely that she did not like or trust Trevor Malcolm. Of course he was far from being a killer, and bore no resemblance to Gyges. Her aversion had nothing to do with the myth or story of Croesus, or with her brief fancy that Trevor represented some sort of danger for Mario. It was that he had shown her his true colours on their walk from Ephesus; and that there had been something forced about last evening. Whatever had possessed her to knock on his door? His other visitor—for whose sake he had glanced two or three times from the window, and tensed on hearing footsteps and voices in the corridor—had never arrived; he'd devoted himself to her alone. He'd played host and been marginally nicer than during their walk, it was true; but there'd been something not quite right about the whole thing—she saw that now; it had been a performance, false, altogether fishy, and it had ended discomfitingly. The sketchbook and tee-shirt with their blood stains (her imagination now worked them to that, in preference to wine), whatever their origin, came like the warning of an Oracle, that she must have no more to do with him.

It's still early, she told herself, swinging out of bed. Why run the risk of bumping into him at breakfast? I'll slip straight out, buy one of those round donut-like things I saw being sold in the street, spend the whole morning at Ephesus looking over the ruins, then catch the bus back to Izmir in the afternoon.

How wonderful not to be tired! Her face in the bathroom mirror swam up looking less grey. She brushed her hair with vigorous strokes and enjoyed the tingling sensation of the bristles on her scalp. 'You don't look unloved,' she confided to the glass and the fleeting imaginary presence of Mario. 'Or unloving. And they say that absence … .'

The morning was glorious and Ephesus hers to ramble in almost alone. She had followed the Arcadian Way to where it submerged itself in the lucent waters of a shallow lake made by the spring rains. Anemones and daisies had yielded to reeds and water lilies, arches and thrusting columns to islanded slabs of marble and sunken marble capitals. From a cloud of mosquitoes occupying a patch of shade made by nearby olive trees came a gentle wailing. And now to her surprise, as she stood still, a chorus swelled and enveloped her; a chorus emanating from frogs—eerie and comical, of mingled sounds suggestive of pixie laughter, a gothic creaking of hinges, hiccoughing and the tensing and twanging of rubber bands. 'You're not like the frogs in my garden at home,' she cried delightedly. At the comment the frogs all fell silent at once. Birds unfamiliar to her skimmed the surface of the water and chased through the reeds; a lizard, half grey, half green—a miniature dinosaur—sunned itself on a marble island.

Returning at length, she paused in what had been the centre of the ancient city, directly below the Great Theatre that nestled on the lower slopes of Mount Pion. Leave the Theatre till last, she thought. From its highest point she would be able to sum up the whole. Her eyes fell on a peacock, crudely incised in one of the paving stones. Greek, Roman, or Christian? A pity she could not be certain about such things, a pity she had not done more than begin to become an archaeologist. She strolled on, the length of the Street of Kuretes, pausing over her Fodo to identify as she passed them the Fountain of Trajan, the Temple of Hadrian with its frieze of Fortune, and the foundations of a row of shops. In the Lower Agora she settled herself on the base of a column and let her eyes rest on the massive chest and abdomen, the worn stone musculature, of a male torso that lay among clumps of daisies. It seemed, briefly, a tragedy the rest of him was missing; and she barely resisted an impulse to kneel and place her hand consolingly on the biceps of the arm nearest. She read of the city's decline, of how the river Cayster had brought silt down from the hills until the harbour had been transformed into marshland, making trade with the world impossible; and how with the marshes and brackish water had come the mosquitoes and malaria.—It was something *he* had mentioned, the mosquitoes, the malaria. She saw the sail-clad little ships, forced to moor further and further from the town, by the lava-like advance of the silt. But the mosquitoes—she shuddered, seeing again the descendants of those mosquitoes, repulsively, bloodily, glued to the walls and ceiling of her room in the Hotel Croesus. From these her thoughts were drawn again to the ominous stains of the tee-shirt and on the pages of the sketchbook in Trevor Malcolm's bathroom.

What had his reaction been on not coming across her at breakfast, or on picking up the plug for his basin—which she had left for Mr Deverli to give him, deliberately with no accompanying note of thanks?

She got up and walked some distance, consulting her guidebook without taking anything in. She recalled Trevor Malcolm, going to the window and glancing down into the street; and his gruff, faintly fevered, talk of the castle and the Temple of Artemis. She had a sudden premonition that things were not finished between them. Only the sight of the Great Theatre and the prospect of ascending its numerous flights of stone steps in the midday sun refocused her mind on present surroundings and restored her to something like her former complacency. She climbed. The great horseshoe curves of the Theatre rippled and surged at her feet, an ocean of stones singing wildly in the glare with cicadas.

On Trevor Malcolm's suddenly stepping into her path as she reached the top of the Theatre she gasped, lost her balance, and was caught and steadied by him.

'Sorry,' he said, before letting her go.

'My God, don't do that!' She tore off her sunglasses to glare at him.

'Didn't mean to scare you. Hope you haven't twisted an ankle, or anything?'

She looked about her and sat down on the top step of the flight she had just climbed. 'No, I'm okay.' She was at once angry with herself, as much as with him, for not being more sorry to see him.

'Good.'

'I'm torn between wanting to slap your face for frightening me like that and—'

'And?'

She glanced back, her eyes losing in spite of herself their hostility. 'And feeling I ought to thank you for saving me from a nasty fall.'

'It's a long climb. And with the sun, one gets dizzy.'

'My legs feel like jelly.'

He nodded. 'Worth it, though. All those stone steps. Fabulous view.'

She replaced her sunglasses. 'I thought you said you'd seen enough of Ephesus and that you didn't want to come back.'

He sat down near her. 'Changed my mind.'—He thought: What would she do if she knew the truth, if she knew I'd returned to Ephesus with the Tourist Police after filing a report with them about a man I killed on this very spot yesterday afternoon?

'I've had a wonderful morning.' She got up. 'I took my time and looked at everything, all by myself.' She wanted the point made clear.

'And now the Theatre, the last and best thing of all.' He rose and with a sweeping gesture took in the descending rows of stone. Looking back at her, intently and in the full sun, he saw her as though for the first time; and saw that she was pretty. It came to him abruptly that she must help him forget his odd morning and the calamity of yesterday afternoon. He badly needed a diversion.

She tilted her face to him with a faintly quivering smile. 'Why *did* you decide to return here?'

'Ah,' he responded, slightly shaking his head. 'Why indeed.'

'Yes, why?' she persisted.

He hesitated, then brought out: 'Because I wanted to see *you* again, that's why!'

They both laughed, she nervously. He knew it was not true; she was tempted, against reason, to think it might be.

'You don't believe me?'

She shook her head, dropping her eyes to the daisies, the anemones, at her feet. 'Not at all.'

'The Theatre's the *pièce de résistance*,' he hurried on. 'So complete, so intact. It doesn't take much to imagine the crowd, twenty-five thousand people, watching something by Euripedes or Plautus, or a couple of gladiators fighting to the death. You know they moved the ladies up here, from the front seats, because they had favourite gladiators, got too excited, and made their husbands jealous.—You can see the whole city, the surrounding hills, almost to the sea. I knew you'd find your way up here eventually. And that's why I came.'

'I wasn't going to miss it. But I never thought that you … after what you said.' She glanced at him quizzically, then looked all severity. 'And as a matter of fact I didn't *want* to see you again.'

'I've been that bad?—Why weren't you at breakfast? I hope you didn't miss it on my account?'

'Of course not. I hardly ever eat breakfast. Anyway, I wouldn't miss it on your account.—And now I've got to go.' Yes, she really must. She meant it. More talk was futile. She'd decided against him; she must stick to it.

'*Go*?' He hid some genuine alarm by a theatrical gesture of dismay, then took a few steps away from her and stood with his hands in his pockets staring disconsolately into the distance. Oddly, he ached to confide in her. He wanted to tell her about his morning, his frustrating, inconclusive morning. But that would be madness, and surely the ultimate in selfishness besides—vile, in fact, to mix her into this mess.

His morning had passed strangely and he'd still been trying to make sense of it when he'd spotted her, far below, ascending the long flight of steps that would bring her, providing she followed them the whole way, precisely to his vantage point at the top of the Theatre. He'd wakened more confident that he was not being pursued by the man climbing the path on Mount Pion, and reproaching himself for having bolted from the body of the man he'd killed, bolted in fear and revulsion; and also guilt, as though he'd done something other than defend himself. Bolted!—without going though the man's pockets and finding out something about him. At breakfast, fidgety, self-critical and deprived of the distraction of Carey, he'd decided there was nothing for it but to return to the scene of the business, which he expected to see cordoned off and crawling with police. He felt even less relish for spending the rest of his life in guilt and ignorance than for entrusting himself to the reputedly untender mercies of the police or Turkey's military authorities. Imperfect human being though he considered himself to be, he divined that he couldn't live with the pretence that nothing had happened. Pleading not guilty before the tribunal of self, he recognised that he required more: a modicum of reassurance of the same from his fellow creatures, some independent acknowledgement of innocence. That was why he'd returned—only to be astonished at finding the place not cordoned off and not crawling with police. Of course the body had been removed, but where was the evidence that there had ever been one? To his admittedly inexpert eyes the spring grass appeared lush and untrampled, the daisies and anemones sprouting between the stones, unbent, unbroken; existing in a day quite beautiful, quite unspoiled, and seeming to declare that nothing unusual had happened there, nothing at all; that the whole affair was a bad dream. He had plunged down the steps and found a public telephone that worked, knowing someone at the offices of the Tourist Police would have at least a rough grasp of English; but the three plain clothes officers arriving in an unmarked car had accompanied him with no obvious sense of purpose up the stairs of the Theatre, listened politely to what he'd had to say, and offered little in the way of comment. He'd been driven to their offices in Selçuk, required to answer a few questions and put his name to a brief report, then courteously returned to Ephesus. Doubt had been expressed as to the victim's having died, a Swiss knife being small, unlikely to have inflicted mortal damage, and Mr Malcolm having left the scene hurriedly and in shock, and without, by his own admission, properly examining him. Perhaps Mr Malcolm was mistaken. The altercation, the struggle, represented a misunderstanding; and what he had said to the man had been taken badly, but at the end of the day, as it were, was it not most probable that the victim had recovered and removed himself, perhaps with the help of the man climbing the path? And the rifle?—Trevor had asked. Turks have them, the officers said; all sorts, left over from the troubles. But what was he doing, this man who died, or did not die?—Adjusting the sights, one of the policemen suggested. There, in the Theatre? A collective shrugging of shoulders sufficiently indicated official refusal to pursue the subject further. The distinct and puzzling impression Trevor had come away with was that these men of the Tourist Police were unwilling to treat the matter seriously, or else were unwilling to let him think that they did.

He turned back to Carey. He must keep her. He saw that clearly. And in order to do so he would have to tell her something of this, at least. 'I'll be nice,' he assured her. 'I've changed.'

She sighed. 'No, really. It doesn't matter if you have. I've got to see about times of buses and so on.'

'I should explain. Yesterday was not a good day. And when you came to my room I was half expecting someone altogether less welcome.'

A woman, she caught herself thinking again. And of course you'd say less welcome

'There was a wee bit of a problem—'

And she hadn't turned up, this woman—she persisted silently. What would've happened if she had? With me there? Was he jittery about that? 'I don't want to know. It doesn't matter. But I must go—.' She fully intended to, certainly; yet she found herself curious to hear his explanation.

'No, you must listen!—You see, I encountered, up here in the Theatre, on this very spot, this objectionable type, this man, and ... we had a bit of a row. I got the better of him, shed blood, in fact. It was all very ... awkward.'

'Blood—' she echoed him.

'Couldn't help it.' He crossed himself and hung his head in mock contrition.

Blood. The stained tee-shirt, the sketchbook. 'You gave him a bloody nose, then?' she said in measured tones, looking hard at him, raising an eyebrow behind her dark glasses.

'That's the idea, yes,' he returned brightly.

'So you were expecting him last night? Thinking he might come back to get even?'

'Was it that obvious?—Sorry. Yes, well—no, not him; his friend, actually. I call him "M," this friend. I wasn't *really* expecting him, because I didn't—and still don't—think he got a good look at me, on that path on Mout Pion. But I was a bit edgy nevertheless.'

'"M"?—why "M"?'

'"M" for Mercedes, the car I think he drives, the one that passed us.' He sought for a way to stop her leaving. 'You say you have to go. But why? there's a *dolmush*—a bus—every couple of hours.' An idea landed. 'You know, you could see Aphrodisias, if you stayed.'

'*Stayed*!' Her eyes behind the sunglasses widened in astonishment.

'You said you were cautious. Well, a body can be too cautious. Change. Surprise yourself. Do something spur-of-the-moment. Live a little. Don't be a stick-in-the-mud.'

She suppressed a smile. Eerily, it was more or less her advice to herself. 'But that's—'

'I thought you said you'd been interested in archaeology.'

'I was; I even began to study it. But staying's quite impossible.'

'Nothing's impossible.'

'Aphrodisias?'

'Yes!'

'But it's nowhere near here, is it?'

'It's not far. You just have to stay another night.'

She laughed outright. Another night! What was the man thinking? That she could ignore what was planned, drop the tour itinerary, give up what they were doing—?

'Nothing's impossible!' he pursued. 'Aphrodisias is pristine, as yet undiscovered by the multitude, unpolluted by the great unwashed.' He was aware that this wasn't what he'd planned for himself, but it would do for now. He dreaded the prospect of the rest of the day, the evening, the night, on his own; tormenting himself about who the dead man was, worrying anew that M might after all be looking for him.

'But I couldn't possibly!—The itinerary's set. My husband went to a lot of trouble—'

'Carey—'

It was the first time he had used her name. In spite of herself she felt a little stab of pleasure.

'I counted on seeing you at breakfast; then I came back here—despite my aversion to the place—just to see you,' he said, continuing the lie and almost believing in it now. 'Listen,' he pursued, searching intently for her eyes behind the sunglasses. 'There's not a bad *locanta*, sort of an open affair, just across and down a few steps from the hotel—'

'*Locanta*?'—why listen to him? she thought. Why even let him finish? Dammit, why am I not telling him to get lost?

'A *locanta*'s a restaurant.' He banished a grin with a shake of his head. 'They serve other things besides nuts and apricots from paper bags. Then tomorrow morning I could show you over Aphrodisias. Seriously, it's the best, the most exciting Classical site in Turkey. Potentially, at least. You won't find anything like it in Greece. And you'd have an expert guide, me. After that I'd get you safely back to Izmir or Boursa or wherever.'

'No,' she said firmly; then made the mistake of explaining. 'The tour I'm on is leaving Izmir tomorrow morning. We're going to be seeing Troy.'

He laughed, without mirth. 'Why, there's nothing left of Troy! Nothing that's authentic, except a few stones scattered about, and a squalid little kiosk or two proffering postcards of Herr Schliemann and Field Marshal Agamemnon!'

She felt her resistance shaken. Byzantine Greece, Christian

Greece, Mario's world of red stone churches with their frescoes and icons, was what she still most eagerly looked forward to; but now she felt the Pagan world beckoning, too. Ephesus had been an eye-opener, awakening an interest that had slumbered since her days as an archaeology student. Musing that it would, perhaps, be a pity to leave Turkey without taking this opportunity to see Aphrodisias, she went doggedly on nevertheless to say that she had paid for the tour and had not the slightest intention of missing any of what was on it.

'Money!' he laughed. 'What's money? Aside from the root of all evil.—Careful, don't step back.' He had advanced, while talking, causing her to retreat to where the stone seats fell away.

Turning from him, she let herself down uncertainly on one of them. She was again aware of a deeply tanned forearm, extending beyond a rolled shirt-sleeve. Her heartbeat seemed irregular, her legs shaky. 'Don't go on,' she implored. But he did go on; she heard him through her rapid thoughts, continuing in the same vein, describing now in more detail the ruins of Aphrodisias, touching on the myths connected with the worship of the great goddess of love, assuring her she would not be disappointed.

'Let me just ... think.' It sounded like defeat. It was defeat. Why delay the surrender? At least it would not be unconditional. A tremor of excitement ran through her, as instantly regretted and denied. Not to do with him, she assured herself. She really was excited—reflecting now—about seeing it. Seeing this new site. Seeing Aprodisias. Being able to tell the people on the tour, tell Gloria. And yet the very name—. She rose slowly and stood staring down into the Theatre, only waiting for him to stop, so she could tell him.

'Well, all right,' she was allowed to say eventually; her tone reluctant, her intention to attach to the consent as many difficulties as she could think of. 'I'll have to re-book the room here, phone the Izmir Palas, tell the tour guide I'll meet up with them in Boursa or Istanbul, arrange about my suitcase, which unfortunately has my passport in it.'

He sighed with relief. The matter was settled. She would stay. 'It'll be easy for you to see to it, the re-booking, phoning, and so forth. Then it's dinner tonight and the city of love tomorrow.'

The city of love—

Across the triumph he scarcely troubled to conceal flitted anew the notion that this was not really what he wanted, not what he'd promised himself at all. It would, however, do for now. A welcome, a necessary, distraction.

She returned his smile and nodded. There would be a night, too; a night, however, which posed no danger. An *affair* was out of the question. There was not the remotest possibility of her hopping into bed with this man. She would keep firmly in mind how disagreeable he could be. He would remain someone she did not like, did not entirely trust. Even if he were otherwise, she could never hurt Mario. She derived satisfaction, thinking that she was—rather unkindly—*using* this stranger. No, she concluded, certainly there would be, after all, no harm in it, no harm in having said yes—yes to the *locanta* this evening, yes to Aphrodisias tomorrow.

But the next moment she saw Mario waving goodbye to her at JFK, blowing kisses, and she felt a flutter of uncertainty. A notion of disloyalty, of betrayal, of guilt. Following Trevor down the scooped stone steps of the Theatre she seemed to be falling after him, her body tumbling to collide with his disastrously on the sunlit marble stage below.

## Chapter 6

'I AM MUSTAFA,' boomed the disarmingly effusive man who welcomed them to the *locanta* that evening, spreading his arms so his sleeves shrank back up them and showed clumps of black hair matted over their podgy whiteness. 'Choose any table—please!' His grin caused for an instant three metallic teeth to trap the last rays of a blood-shot sun. Carey and Trevor settled at the side of the room that partially opened to the street and a section of pavement where more tables were set up.

She brushed a few overlooked crumbs from her place. 'Looks like there's just us.'

'Ah, you spoke too soon.' He jerked his head, guiding her to a slightly stooping man in a baggy black suit who had just come in. 'How about *rakis* for starters?'

'Sure.' Wondering what these were, she frowned her way through a menu holding the promise of 'Nightingale's Nests,' 'Lover's lips' and 'Lady's Thighs.'

'Shall I choose?—Octopus salad, pilav, kebab, a bottle of Doluca, for example?'

'Super.'

While Mustafa took the order from Trevor, her thoughts strayed to Mr Deverli, dialing for her with hs furry fingers the number of the Izmir Palas. Busy, busy and still busy. She must remember to try again; Kadir had still to be told not to expect her till Istanbul.

Their rakis arrived. A first sip made Carey cough.

'Rough stuff, but good, eh?—Well, here's more company!'

Two ancient diesel vans had noisily and malodorously pulled up at the curb beyond the outside tables; and now, from the first of these, several young men tumbled—to swing open the rear doors of the second, and reveal, seated on side benches within, a dozen old men, clutching rifles between their knees; and, on the floor, two enormous dogs of indeterminate breed, guarding a dead and blood-caked wild boar lying between them. The van doors, the youths waiting respectfully on either side, framed a singular picture. As Carey and Trevor watched, the old men solemnly stowed their rifles and descended. Mustafa loudly greeted them, pumped the hands of some, embraced others, and with two waiters effected the reorganization of all the small square tables on the pavement into a long table for each of the generations. The waiters vanished and within moments reappeared bearing copper trays laden with large and small glasses, bottles of beer and raki.

'Now you wouldn't see that on your tour,' was Trevor's comment.

She readily agreed. The scene recalled some painting, a Teniers perhaps; or else, more all-inclusively, the divided chorus of a Greek tragedy, herself and Trevor the protagonists. She tried the raki again and managed not to cough.

Trevor signaled one of the young waiters to bring the Doluca. He was bent on enjoying himself. So what if he'd planned something altogether different, his Oriental Experience, *an affaire à la turque*, in Istanbul or Ankara, if not in the country. This American was not at all his cup of *çai,* but she was, undeniably, pretty; and now, in her company, he might begin to thrust from his mind what had happened at Ephesus. Already the identity of the dead man didn't matter so much, and with each passing minute it seemed more certain that the man climbing the path on Mount Pion did not intend to come after him.

Carey listened while he enthused about south-western Turkey, described its archaeological sites and treasures. He spoke leaning forward, smiling slightly, his eyes on hers. She told him about the male torso and the peacock at Ephesus, and about the frog chorus in the swamp. She began to enjoy herself. She felt exhilarated at the novelty of everything. It was partly the strong red wine, combining agreeably with the considerably stronger raki. She was amused that their meal consisted of numerous courses, each small, delicately prepared. A slice of lemon seemed to appear with everything. When the plates were removed Mustafa presented them with steaming towels, then sprayed their outsretched hands with Cologne.

As the wine, the raki, worked on them both, they gave little heed to where the topics they embarked on might lead.

'The religion of my friends, the Greeks and Romans,' Trevor was saying, 'all that confusing mythology of squabbles, seductions, gods and goddesses consumed with lust and jealousy, tends to be regarded as frivolous nonsense; an incomprehensible blot on their escutcheon of achievements—epic and lyric poetry, tragedy and comedy, schools of philosophy and science. Yet there's a lot to be said for it.'

'Really?' She startled herself with the notion that if he slightly extended his hand across the table her own could be taken—like the queen in a game of chess.

He nodded vigorously. 'Oh yes. No sacred book, no unique validity or dogma; hence no heresy, no burnings at the stake. No gloomy preoccupation with sin and sex, either. And no priests to tell you what you could and could not read or think about.'

'No priests?—but priest*esses*, then. Like the Oracle at Delphi.'

'They were lay people, ordinary citizens working part-time. There was no class or caste.'

She could not argue the point.

'The one stumbling block for them was the Christians, coming along and insisting on a single deity. I take it you're religious. A good Christian?'

'A Christian, certainly.'

'And Mario?'

'He's Catholic. A *good* Catholic. And he's influenced me—although I've never quite gone over.'

'But you're religious.' He looked mischief: '*And* superstitious, I'll be bound?'

Not wishing to risk ridicule by admitting she'd consulted a medium before deciding on the trip, she merely smiled.

'"A soothsayer bids you beware the Ides of March," he gruffly intoned. 'Brutus to Caesar, isn't it?'

'And Caesar was stabbed, wasn't he?' she riposted. 'Shakespeare's soothsayers were generally right, I seem to remember.'

'Well, as a Christian you've got a few things in common with the old Pagans, anyway. For Mary read Artemis, the mother goddess of Ephesus; for Christ read Apollo; for the Devil read Pan. Even the iconography suggests parallels and borrowings too close to shog off—'

'Stop!' she laughed. 'Cut it out!' Glancing aside, she caught the lone diner staring at her.

'Something wrong?'

'No, nothing.' The man, after all, had no one else to look at except the waiters.

'Being religious, or superstitious,' he went on, 'believing things which have no basis in fact, you risk pressuring them to come true, just by thinking enough about them.'

'Yes,' she concurred musingly. 'Like—'

'Like?'

She had drunk enough to make her put aside a little what she had decided about him. 'Like something you told me about Croesus, which made me associate my husband with him and with what happened to him.'

He did not, could not, know what she meant. 'I see,' he said nevertheless.

'So I'll stop thinking like that.'

'Oh, by the way, I've remembered something about the story: the woman was the one behind the murder. Her quirky husband wanted his friend and bodyguard, Gyges, to see how beautiful she was and arranged for him to spy on her naked, which was a no-no with goddesses and queens in those days. She discovered the connivance, gave Gyges a dagger and made him choose either to kill her husband and take over the kingdom and her along with it, or kill himself.'

'You say the woman, but it was Gyges, who did … kill her husband and take over the kingdom and her along with it.'

'So they say.'

Awaiting coffee they looked up to see one of the party of hunters, a tall solemn-faced young man, standing beside them. 'If you please,' he said hesitantly, 'my Uncle sends to ask if you would be so kind as to sit with us and take a glass of raki?'

Trevor hid some slight irritation behind a polite assent. Carey was torn between regret that their *tête-à-tête* was ended, and relief that what she perceived as a growing threat of intimacy posed by its continuance need not now concern her. They scrambled up. Room was made for them and for the messenger, Hasan, at the table of the elder hunters. The young man explained that all the men of their party were tobacco farmers who had nothing to do at present since planting would not occur until May, and that they came from Torbali, a village inland from Izmir. 'This is my Uncle,' he went on, with a respectful nod towards the head of the table, where an old man with features gnarled like a *wurzelmensch* presided. 'He is eighty-three.' The men on either side of the Uncle were introduced: the first being described as the Neighbour—with whom, they gathered, the Uncle frequently quarreled good-naturedly; and the other, designated the Oil Wrestler (long since retired but still respectfully remembered as such). Nods and grins sufficed for the rest, while raki was hastily poured and glasses raised. The old men were eager to know about their guests and had drunk enough to make them bold in questioning. Conversation soon became chaotic. Hasan, as translator, could not accommodate the curiosity of more than one at a time; so that others, wanting to question but left out, anxious to follow but unable to understand, or failing to hear, fell to questioning their neighbours or commenting impatiently among themselves on the proceedings.

In the midst of this hubbub Carey remembered she had still to phone Kadir at the Izmir Palas, whispered urgently to Trevor, and managed simultaneously to catch the sleeve of Mustafa, just then bringing the bottle of raki with which Trevor intended to match the old hunters' generosity. Led inside, she tried to collect her thoughts while Mustafa dialed for her. The wine and raki made her head spin. She considered what the other members of the tour might be saying about her staying over in Selçuk; what Gloria, for instance, might be thinking and saying—Gloria Bloomquist, who must resent having no one in the next bed to listen to the stream of little complaints that had already begun with the Turkish plane from London; complaints about the grittiness of the coffee, the sickly sweetness of the dessert, the scarcity of ice for her Manhattan. A moment's imperfect reflection brought Carey to the confident conclusion that she could not be harmed by Gloria's speculations, or those of anyone else on the tour. They were false, if they existed. She could deny them with a clear conscience. They would never get to Mario, never hurt him.

Mustafa handed her the receiver and bowed his way back down the corridor. A faint and crackling 'Hello' came: Kadir's voice.

'Hi, Kadir!—It's me, Mrs Signorello in Selçuk. I'm staying away another couple of days. Can you hear?—Meet you all in Istanbul, at the Hilton.—Oh, and Kadir? There are a few things out in my room—nightdress and so on—if you'd just ask Mrs Bloomquist to stuff them back in my suitcase and then bring the suitcase? And I'll see you at the hotel in Istanbul, the Hilton—okay?'

'I understand, Mrs Signorello.'

'My passport is there, too. In the side pocket of the suitcase. Very important. So take good care of it, okay?'

'Passport, yes of course.'

'You got the message I left at the desk last night, that I was staying on here?'

'Yes, as soon as we arrived back. I guess you enjoy yourself?'

'Yes, I'm having dinner with some wild boar hunters.'

'I beg your pardon?'

'Boar hunters—you know, pig, wild pig.'

'Sorry?'

'Never mind.—But Kadir, tell me something: why did you take off without me from Ephesus? Why didn't you get the driver to honk, like you said? I mean it worked out, but it might not have. I was really scared for a while. Didn't you realise I hadn't come back, or what?'

Silence met this.

Carey repeated the question. What excuse was he trying to dream up? She heard him clear his throat and resume in a voice that sounded hesitant and hurt:

'Perhaps you are joking with me, Mrs Signorello—'

She denied it.

'But your friend—?'

'Friend?'

'Yes, yes—At Ephesus, your friend.'

'What friend, Kadir? I don't understand.'

'There was a message, you know, from your friend.'

*Trevor*! she thought, and flushed with indignation. My friend! Trevor Malcolm!

'A boy brought me the message from him, and so we left. We didn't wait any more.—Hello? Mrs Signorello?'

'Yes, I'm here.—So you left.' God, she thought, it was all *his* doing. Trevor's little plot. Perhaps she ought to feel flattered, but the underhandedness of it and the recollection of those first panic-stricken moments in the parking lot made her angry with him.

'But surely, Mrs Signorello, that is what you wished?' Kadir pressed on. 'And you friend will return you to us. Is that not correct?'

She pretended it was, but contrived to make him explain further. A boy, a Turkish boy, had brought the message, calling her by name. She had met a friend and this friend would drive her back to Izmir. The bus should not wait. She thanked Kadir and hung up.

Who but Trevor? Who but him? Because there was no one else. No one at all. She had no 'friend' in Turkey.

Another explanation, namely that Kadir had fabricated the tale of the boy and his message to mask some form of his own incompetence, she could discount at once. Even if he hadn't made an accurate head-count, Gloria and the others would have let him know she was missing. The bus would not have been allowed to leave the parking lot unless there were some different, reasonable and widely shared understanding. She must conclude that Kadir was telling the truth. A message definitely had been delivered. Someone, her 'friend,' had deliberately *arranged* to have her stranded in Ephesus, and had schooled the messenger in what he was to tell Kadir. And that friend was Trevor Malcolm, the man taking her to dinner, returning with her to the hotel, possibly expecting to go to bed with her. And what else? she asked herself in mounting alarm—to kidnap me, demand ransom money from Mario?

She supposed he had seen her earlier by chance, learned her name (overheard it or got it from the bus driver), then paid a boy to deliver the message so she would be left stranded in the parking lot looking out for help as he conveniently passed by. The elaborateness of the plan, the energy that must have been put into it, chilled her. All Trevor's reluctance, his offhandedness, his irritation, on meeting and escorting her to Selçuk was feigned, then—all planned. Even the diversion of the story of the 'scrap' in the Theatre at Ephesus, the stained tee-shirt and sketchbook (wine-stains, after all), deviously, cunningly, arranged!

And his motive was not merely to seduce her, surely. It must be something more, much more. To do with her money. Mario's fortune.

And yet—

Wishing she had drunk less of the raki, less of the wine, she redoubled her effort to recall events and to think clearly. No one, as yet, had entered the corridor to disturb her.

Objections now crowded in. What sort of planning was this, she soon found herself asking, when he could leave her to wait for a bus that would have taken her away if she herself had not decided to do something else? It was true he'd suggested she stay over in Selçuk, but the tone had been flippant; he hadn't tried to persuade her. Reconsidering his initial belligerence, his air of apparently desperate preoccupation, she came up against further difficulties. *She'd* been the one who had knocked on his door at the hotel last night. She saw his look of surprise, then his furtive glances from the window, which had led her to believe his real interest lay in the arrival of someone else.

These odd and conflicting considerations passed before her like incidents or scenes in a play that might well have been in Turkish. She was left in total confusion. All she could think, however, was that Trevor Malcolm *must* have been the 'friend.' Simply because there was no one else. She came back to that. She didn't understand, but would do well to regard him as dangerous and to drop him as quickly as possible. It was surely the safest thing. Of course the evening must be gone through, up to the moment of a polite good-night outside the door of her room at the Croesus. She would hide her indignation, hide the burden of her telephone conversation with Kadir. There was no saying what he would do if he knew his plan had failed. She resolved to find out from Mr Deverli the times of buses and escape first thing in the morning.

## Chapter 7

SHE RETURNED TO the table wearing a set smile for those whose tumblers were raised to welcome her back. 'Kadir's a talker,' she said apologetically.

'We're onto politics. And war.'

*War*?—surely the possibility was remote. Mario had said so. Mr Deverli, too.

But no. War, it seemed, could come at any moment. 'Now it's seismic operations,' Hasan was explaining. 'The Greeks have no right to do this, you see. It is, as my Uncle says, in violation of the Bern Agreement.'

'We are warriors'—such was the old Oil Wrestler's opinion; the Greeks should not forget it. The Greeks are crafty devils, the Neighbour put in; a servile race, fit only to be ruled, and the Turks were their natural masters and should rule over all the Greek lands again as they had in days past. But the Uncle held up his hand and spoke softly: The great days of empire were gone. Besides, the Greeks were not so bad; not all of them. (This was generous, daring, and briefly reduced the others to shocked silence.) Precipitate action now might irreparably harm Turkey's reputation among civilized nations. There was the respect of the world to consider. Loans to be negotiated, too. The Neighbour objected, and spat. Words flowed from him which Hasan did not trouble to translate. Tension between the Neighbour and the Uncle mounted; the others fell silent, their heads turning, tennis-game-like, to the one and then the other until general laughter at the Neighbour's memory failing him on a vital point dispelled it.

Trevor swayed gently in his place, his thoughts side-tracked by these tales of old wrongs and triumphs, seemingly the sad proofs of a deathless hatred.

Glancing aside at him, Carey thought: I could almost take him for a Turk, if I had chanced on this gathering and didn't know. Dark, like them. All he needs is a droopy black moustache.—Feeling herself isolated, a woman at a table full of men, a hostage of Turks, she looked away for relief; only to have her eye fall on the blood-caked boar, which, from between the open doors of the nearest van, seemed to be staring balefully back at her.

Unaware of the change she had undergone, he slipped his arm around her shoulders—only to have it gently but firmly removed.

A bogus archaeologist? she wondered. Even *that* planned so we'd appear to have something in common to start us off? He knew my name before we met in the parking lot, got the boy to tell Kadir.—She was angry at being taken for a fool.

And yet—

Her need to be alone, to think things through, had become almost unbearable. And now there was war to worry about, war at any moment. Around her the voices, strange utterance, words of shadowy import, murmured and rose, clashed and trailed off disquietingly, infuriatingly, into the darkness.

Holding her in his gaze the Uncle mumbled something. Hasan brushed away an apologetic cough. 'My Uncle says our conversation must be boring to a lady. He says he has seen your thoughts flying afar like flakes from a fire.'

'The raki,' said Carey, smiling wanly. 'It is good but strong. I'm not used to it.'

The Uncle nodded, evidently pleased to hear she thought the raki strong. His eyes shone with a kindly light, then to her relief left her. The conversation was turned by the Uncle along domestic paths. Women in the villages of Anatolia, he observed, lead the lives of their mothers and grandmothers and lack the freedom of the women of Istanbul and Ankara. Here, the old ways prevail. Husbands and lovers look to their womenfolk for comfort—and for advice, on many matters; but they guard them jealously, and when they work away from their villages sometimes things happen in their absence or are thought to happen. The knife has done terrible things in dark Anatolia! And does so still. Every village draws a veil over its secrets. The Oil Wrestler nodded: yes, the outside world cannot be blamed, for there was always jealousy in Turkish men. Were Turkish men not the proudest among their sex? And perhaps with justification! The best fighting men, the most virile—and naturally the most jealous. It was true, the old man at the far end of the table piped in a voice that was ironically near that of a woman's, while slumped down in his chair so that his chin and beard brushed the bowl in front of him; and there was a time when corpses bobbed as thick as leaves in the morning sunlight on the waters of the Bosphorous and the Golden Horn.

'And polygamy?' asked Trevor, disliking the subject of knives and stabbing.

Laughter. A general stirring and shifting of chairs.

'My Uncle has two wives,' Hasan explained, smiling. 'The others only one. It is not so common now. Few can afford more than one.'

Suddenly it occurred to Carey that she might leave tonight, leave soon—with these men.

'So you plan to see Aphrodisias?' Hasan was asking her.

'Perhaps—' she began hesitantly; telling herself at the same time: I must ask them, ask Hasan. Would they take me? Somehow I must get them to take me—rather than risk another night at the hotel with that man. 'Aphrodisias? No, no,' she said, drawing abruptly nearer and lowering her voice. 'As a matter of fact, just now I ... received some bad news on the telephone, news which changes all that.' She thought quickly. 'I must go back before, you see. To Izmir. Tonight, if possible. I have not yet told my ... friend.' She paused. Her fingers toyed nervously with the paper table cloth until they tore it.

'Tonight?—But there is almost certainly no *dolmush* tonight.'

She looked at him in mute appeal, then glanced down and waited for him to say what she hoped to hear.

'We go to Torbali, our village. It is, I mentioned to you earlier, close to Izmir. From Torbali there are frequent trains.'

'Hasan, could I go with you, go in one of the vans? Would it be possible? Would there be room?' Her eyes flashed hope.

'It might not be comfortable; and with the dogs, the smell—'

On her other side Trevor had risen and was concerning himself with the probable location of the *tuvalet*. He noticed one of the young men returning to the other table, with his hand still on his crotch. 'The time has come,' he announced shortly. 'Back in a minute.'

Ignorant of the arrangement Carey was negotiating with Hasan, he picked his way between the empty tables until he gained the passageway leading to a room that evidently had been tacked on as an afterthought to the main building; a dank, dimly lit room, where there was an open, key-hole shaped toilet in the floor, a long metal trough suspended from the wall, a basin, and the sound of constantly trickling water. Ventilation and a view out into the night was afforded by a space left between the top of the wall, which came only to eye level, and the corrugated metal roof, which was supported by bricks placed at intervals along the top of the wall. He stood there, swaying slightly, taking care not to come in contact with the wet concrete or the edge of the rust-rimmed trough. Looking out, he could see that the *tuvalet* gave onto a *cul de sac*. He finished and went to wash his hands. Something, however, returned him to the space in the wall, and his eyes probed until they made out a slow-moving shape: a vehicle without lights, backing into the *cul de sac* from the main street. He waited, heard the engine die, saw the driver's head and shoulders silhouetted. His heart beat faster. The car was a Mercedes estate. In the dark it might have been any light colour but he had no doubt it was yellow; and that it was the car he'd seen in the parking lot at Ephesus and then passing on the road to Selçuk. The driver remained at the wheel. Seconds turned to minutes. The fellow intended to sit there.

Trevor's throat had gone dry. He fought to keep down his fear and think clearly. The *cul de sac* lay nearly opposite the Hotel Croesus and offered an unobstructed view of its entrance. He told himself that proximity to the *locanta*, the front of which lay around the corner, didn't mean that the man knew his present whereabouts. The bastard had only just parked, and must have been somewhere else when he and Carey had crossed from the hotel; he hadn't seen him, or else he would have acted before this.

Trevor admitted to himself he was scared; yet his recent intake of wine and raki fortified him to some extent. The chance discovery in itself brought satisfaction. The connection between this individual in the old yellow Mercedes and the man he'd left dead in the Theatre was now beyond doubt; as was the danger now facing him. To be the intended victim of someone who must be supposed the vengeful friend of a hit-man wasn't in itself a comforting notion, yet he felt a certain elation. For the time being, at least, he, and not M, was in control.

He made his way back to the table, settled himself and awaited an opportunity to tell his companion what he had seen. Before he could disclose his news to her, however, she turned to him with hers: Gloria Bloomquist had broken her ankle, Carey's presence was required, if only for moral support; Hasan would take her in his van with the hunters to Torbali tonight, and from there she would be catching one of the frequent trains to Izmir. She was sorry, very sorry, but he must see there was nothing she could do about it.

He pondered this. It was a blow. Or it would have been. But

what he'd just seen changed things. 'So that's your news,' he replied at last. 'Well, I've got news too.'

Now what? she wondered, on her guard, sitting forward with her hands on her knees, her knees tightly together.

'The man in the yellow Mercedes, the man I call M, is waiting for me in the street beside us.'

She sharply drew breath. So Trevor thinks he's going to follow me!—she leapt to conclude. This is what he's come up with! I tell him I'm leaving and he has to dream up something fast.—Her look was one of incredulity, then scorn—scorn she did not trouble to hide. 'Waiting for you!'

'Yes. Luckily, I saw him—from the whatsit. And he hasn't seen me.'

'Where—'

'There, through that wall.' Her look baffled him. 'Carey, what the hell's wrong? You don't believe me?'

'I—no, quite frankly.'

'Why not? I don't understand.'

Bastard, she thought. Dissembling, slippery bastard!

'Carey, what's up? What's the matter with you?'

'Keep your voice down.'

Frustrated, uncomprehending, he instantly lost patience, wanted to be rid of her. Rid of her, every bit as much as in the parking lot at Ephesus. She was in the way. Didn't the woman realise his life was in danger after all? How could she be so stupid as not to understand what he'd just told her in plain English?

'I want to look.'

He gripped her arm, tugged her to face him. 'No!—You can't!'

'Do you mind?'

'Yes, dammit, I do mind!' he hissed.

She locked eyes with him fiercely. It was a lie. Another lie. Meant to distract her, make her leave off questioning him in light of what he must have known Kadir had told her on the phone just now. She felt she must act, take up arms against him. To hell with understanding.

'You can't because he may have seen us together,' he continued rapidly. 'He'd come straight in here, find me, finish me off.'

'He doesn't exist!'

'He *bloody does*!'

'Your're hurting—!'

He let her go, as Hasan turned back and began to relay in

translation the Uncle's answers to several questions she had asked earlier.

'I can't stay on here,' Trevor muttered during the next interval of Turkish. 'I must leave the hotel, leave Selçuk. And tonight.—Hasan!'

She watched, angry, fascinated, as he spoke animatedly, in low tones to Hasan.—Really, the lengths to which the man would go, the duplicity, the act he was putting on!—She noted Hasan's expression change, saw him listen intently, nod, smile, nod more vigorously. At one point Hasan laughed outright. At last Hasan rose and went to speak quietly to the Uncle. The Uncle inclined his head then burst out in a flow of words and laughter.

A few minutes later Trevor found an opportunity to whisper harshly: 'They've said yes. They'll smuggle me into one of the vans and drive me to Torbali.'

'Along with me!'

'With or without you.'

'It won't get you anywhere.'

He set his teeth and glanced at her in near hatred. 'It'll get me to Torbali and then to Izmir! And if that's what you've arranged for your sweet self you'll just have to get used to the idea that I'm going too!'

'I suppose you told them you had to *protect* me!'

'Carey, I don't understand. And frankly—'

'I think you understand. But it won't do you any good!'

The woman was maddening—maybe the raki—he could not take time to fathom her mood. She wasn't worth bothering about.

'I suppose you told them—'

'I told them there's a jealous husband after me—*yours*! All that talk about jealousy and stabbing earlier on gave me the idea. So now the only problem is getting our stuff from the hotel—my papers, passport, sketch-book, especially—and paying our bills.'

'I've left nothing. It's with me.'

'Well, good for you.'

She thought grimly: tit for tat, a lie for a lie—hers about Gloria, countered by his about the man in the Mercedes. Then another, for the hunters, about the jealous husband. He meant to follow her. He wasn't going to give up. What had she run into?—This man was intent on harassing her, *stalking* her! Sensing the onset of something like hysteria, she sought to calm herself. She would be rid of him at Izmir. He wouldn't succeed with her, he wouldn't get anywhere with her, once she had made connection with the tour members again, her own people. People from home. She could be back at the Izmir Palas in time to collect her suitcase and passport and leave with the tour in the morning. She could lose him then for sure. 'You'll leave money for the rooms?' she asked, opening her purse, then closing it, thinking how little cash she now had left.—Why give him anything, when he was doing this to her?

'Of course. What do you think I am?'

She might as well have told him. Ignoring her advice to herself she had broken cover and attacked. It was open warfare now. Like Greece and Turkey. She had found it impossible to dissemble. Impossible. Angrily, she watched him explain his mission to Hasan and start off.

The yellow Mercedes didn't exist. It wasn't there. She could be certain it wasn't. And equally certain Trevor's life would not be endangered merely by the simple act of her rising and walking to the end of the room and peering around the open outside wall into the side street to see for herself. Still, she remained where she was and let several minutes pass, managing now to regain some semblance of calm, before she seized the opportunity of a lull in the conversation to get up and go to look.

To her grim satisfaction the yellow Mercedes was indeed not there. The *cul de sac* lay in darkness, empty.

## Chapter 8

SLIPPING OUT THE far side of the *locante* he put what he deemed a safe distance between himself and the Mercedes before crossing the main road, starting back for the hotel, and, in the last of the regions of gloom separating the few dimly glowing street lamps, halting, with the pale hulk of the Croesus rearing itself some twenty metres further on—twenty metres that would bring him in line with the *cul de sac* and the Mercedes, twenty metres that could be his last.

He made up his mind to try the garden—a small square garden surrounded by a low brick and concrete wall, along the top of which ran rusted iron fencing; reasoning that once over and safe from the road he could rap on the garden door or a window and that Mr Deverli or his wife would hear him. The same story he'd told Hasan and the boar hunters about a jealous husband would do for them. A part of the wall next the street but blocked from it by the terminating arch of the aqueduct into which the front of the hotel was built served his purpose. Pulling himself up, he drew breath, flattened himself against the sloping stonework of the aqueduct, and swiveled gingerly inwards—only to stare in astonishment; for framed in the lighted window opposite stood a bed sagging beneath the weight of Mr Deverli and a female companion, both naked; he sitting astride his supine consort, absently kneeding her breasts while watching a small black and white television on which a football game flickered. Regarding the curvature of Mr Deverli's considerable belly, Trevor marveled that the woman he straddled could still breathe. The man's sagging buttocks seemed in their flopping overlap to be on the point of running down both sides of the body beneath like duck fat.

What now?—To disturb the riggish hotelier and his friend would be to risk mayhem. He moved out slightly and surveyed the arch and wall above. The stones of the arch offered toe holds and the arch itself protection from the road. Soon he was working his way upwards, wedging himself in the space between the arch and the front of the hotel. Slow work, since the narrowness of the space all but prevented him from bending his legs. Watched with apparent unconcern by the stork Carey had seen the night before, in its nest some metres distant, he clawed, rested, toiled on, until he came level with a window and was able to crawl inside. Congratulating himself on his room key's being in his pocket, he stood breathless but triumphant in the upstairs corridor.

Moments later, having stuffed his few belongings into his backpack, he was returning the way he had come; more slowly and painstakingly, burdened and with the backpack snagging frequently on the stonework. He retreated along the street until it seemed safe to cross.

It was at this point that an odd and unnerving thing happened.

He had stepped from the curb when he found himself pinned by the suddenly switched up headlights of an approaching car. It was too late to step back into the shadows he had emerged from. The car stopped to allow him to cross in front of it. Shakily he did so. Gaining the opposite curb and the far shadows, he glanced at the car as it slipped past; and, to his astonishment, saw that it was the Mercedes estate!

Trevor's reappearance interrupted Carey's turning over in her mind—but not finally deciding—that she must try to convince Hasan he wasn't to be trusted and deserved to be left behind.

'I left enough money and a note for Deverli, and I've got everything,' she heard him mutter. 'But a funny thing happened. Tell you when we get going.'

An immediate recounting proved impossible, however, the Uncle insisting on the status of each as a guest, who was not to be seated in the rear of a van among men and dogs and bad smells but in a place of honour in accordance with the laws of hospitality; and as there was only one bucket seat, apart from the driver's, in each of the cabs, this meant Carey's being taken into the cab of the van driven by the Uncle and containing members of the older generation and Trevor's being taken into the cab of the van driven by Hasan and containing the younger crowd—with as much merry secrecy and diversion as members of the entire boar hunting contingent, in varying degrees of intoxication, could muster.

The vans started up and accelerated into the night. The lights of the town gave way to a winding road and overarching darkness.

The Uncle puttered along in front; Hasan hung back a respectful distance. Now and then the Uncle glanced zestfully aside at Carey, bursting out with something—a feature of the landscape, an anecdote connected with a village they were passing through. Aware that she understood not a word, he ventured to say that he thought he ought to want to make love to her, if only he were forty or fifty years younger; but that in fact he had forgotten precisely why the act was so important and had been so pleasurable. To all of this she replied with a smile in the darkness, or a nod. As soon as she thought it polite to do so, she closed her eyes, pretended to doze, while her imagination painted the scenes she had missed by not going on the bus with the others today: a journey to Cesme, hot sulphur springs, beaches lapped by the turquoise waves of the Aegean, sights of Izmir which were to have included a bazaar, a mosque, a museum, night life. Tomorrow morning the tour was to depart from Izmir for Istanbul, visiting Pergamum and Troy on the way. She rejoiced to think she would be with them. Trevor had described Troy as 'a few stones.' She didn't trust him on that either, now. She wanted to see for herself. She wanted even more to get away safely, and as soon as possible, *from him.*

Her thoughts reverted to the immediate future and the next stage of the journey to Izmir. They were to catch a train at Torbali, a village not far from Izmir, Hasan had said. She was beyond being curious to know what it was Trevor had to tell her, the 'funny thing' he'd mentioned. Instead she worried that she was to be left with him again for a time, in the station at Torbali and on the train—not alone, she hoped. By then she would be even more tired and vulnerable than she was now. She must fend him off, by whatever means; even if she had to scream for help, even if she had to attack him with her nails.

Assured they were not being followed, Trevor, alert in the cab of the trailing van, had settled down to questioning Hasan about terrorism in the country, how much of it there still was. The military had cracked down on political assassination, certainly, but censorship meant some incidents went unreported, incidents between rival gangs or within the ranks of the Turkish Mafia, incidents involving foreign governments who chose Turkey as a conveniently turbulent place in which to act against their own or rival nationals. A diplomat selling secrets, a trade commissioner taking kick-backs, even an outspoken opposition politician, might still be disposed of, and without fuss. Only the other day there had been something involving an Arab diplomat—Hasan could not recall it precisely, but something of the sort. Trevor hid the intensity of his interest on hearing this, allowing several minutes to pass before reverting to the subject—only to learn that the killing had taken place, not in Ephesus but in Ankara.

Some minutes of silence between them followed, broken by Hasan's inquiring: 'Have you known Mrs Signorello for long?'

'A couple of days.'

Hasan laughed. 'I see. What a pity she has a husband. You are very nice together.'

'Nice together? Really? You think so?—Funny you should say that, because I've got the impression she can't wait to get rid of me.'

Hasan glanced aside in disbelief.

'We were doing fine, but then she changed.'

'Not, I hope, because of us? My uncle?—We were all very—'

'No, no. It was the phone call she made. Something to do with the phone call. Maybe she caught some flack from one her friends for leaving the tour she was on and decided to blame me for leading her astray.'

'Ah, you led her astray—'

'As far as I could, which wasn't far.'

He watched the pools of light from the headlamps glancing away towards the black sky, now, as the van climbed; then, again, dropping to make the asphalt glitter. He realised that the red glow from the tail lights of the van in front had grown fainter. 'You've slowed,' he remarked.

'There is, now, a vehicle behind us,' Hasan replied. 'Quite far. Evidently he has no wish to pass.'

'He won't pass?'

'Probably he is afraid to. Late at night, two vans, the road quite narrow.'

'Probably.' Trevor said this, though by no means reassured.

Shortly after two o'clock a sprinkling of lights announced the town of Torbali. The vans caught one another up and halted outside a square stone building.

'The railway station,' Hasan unnecessarily informed his companion.

'And the vehicle that was tailing us?'

'He was still there, until a few minutes ago.'

'Still there—'

Hasan laughed. 'But he stopped or turned off. You are nervous of the husband, but probably it was not him at all.'

Trevor alighted, stiff and with renewed pain in his neck and shoulder. Carey was already thanking everyone and saying goodbye. Left alone together, the two of them watched the tail lights of the vans dim and disappear in the darkness, then turned wordlessly and entered the dreary waiting room.

## Chapter 9

FINDING NO ONE at the ticket counter he called through to a faintly illuminated inner office but was not answered. He pushed open the door to the platform and stared for a time at the lines of track glistening in the light of a three-quarter moon.

'Hasan was sure there would be trains!' she said exasperatedly. 'Why isn't there at least someone here?'

'It's a bit early, after all.' He turned back and began studying a faded timetable on the wall.

'There must be something coming,' she persisted petulantly, almost past caring that she found herself alone with him after all. 'Hasan couldn't be that wrong. Maybe we're supposed to buy a ticket on the train.'

'Nothing till 7.40,' he announced. 'Of course this thing's probably out of date. It looks it.'

'7.40! But then I'll miss them! That's too late!' Mistrustful, she joined him to scan the timetable. 'Show me where it says 7.40.'

He jabbed his finger at the faded entry. 'And it's a *posta*, an old steam job, the slowest kind—rather than a fast diesel *mototrens*. Still, don't despair. It couldn't be much more than half an hour to Izmir from here.' He wanted to know what had set her against him. His glance, a glance that invited an explanation, and some measure of peace between them, was lost on her. 'So you're set on rejoining your silly tour, are you? For good, I mean.'

'Yes, of course. And it's not a silly tour.'

'To me it is. I'm not a sheep.'

'Neither am I!'

'Rejoining it … for good.' The picture of her on the tour raised his scorn anew. All those sheep, baa-ing their way through this beautiful country; led by Kadir, the guide, 'dressed in a little brief authority.'

'I must.' She got hold of herself, heaved a long sigh. 'Gloria—'

She would try to be nice to him, polite at any rate. She deemed it safer.

'Was that true, about your pal Gloria?' he cut in. It was more an accusation than a question, and without waiting for an answer he stalked to the door by which they had entered and peered up and down the moonlit road.

It was too difficult, after all, to be nice to him. And just not worth it. Tired and cross, she blurted: '*No*! No, it's not! It's not true, about Gloria. It's not, and I don't care!'—She felt herself dangerously close to hysteria.

He returned.

'*You've* lied and so *I've* lied,' she drove on recklessly. 'I've had to, to give you your own back—And to fend you off.'

'*Fend me off*?' he spluttered in disbelief.

'Yes!'

'To fend me off?' he repeated, anger now getting the better of all curiosity, all bewilderment.

Backed against the wall, she could get no further from him. 'Stay away from me!'

'Christ! he said, shaking his head and flinging off to perch on the wooden bench farthest from her. 'I will. I sure as hell will.'

Trembling, she warily watched him—while telling herself: He wouldn't actually attack me. He wouldn't.

Despondently, he returned her stare for a minute or so, until it crossed his mind to ask: 'That phone call you made—?'

She let herself down on the bench nearest her.

'What was it?' he continued. 'What did that guide tell you? What was it, exactly? Everything changed after that. You changed.'

'I found out from Kadir,' she said, striving to control the tremor in her voice, 'that it was you who let the tour bus go, you who told the boy to say that to Kadir.' She struggled to stare down, to meet with contempt, the other's look of apparent astonishment and the burst of mirthless laughter that followed it. 'He said *a friend*,' she continued, only slightly unnerved, 'because he didn't see you, didn't know your name. A friend. All he saw was the boy, your messenger. But I know this friend was you, must have been you.'

'Me? Must have been me?'

'*Yes*!'

'Why?' he shot at her viciously, instantly on his feet again. '*Why*?'

'Because there's no one else!'

He groaned and clutched his head in both hands, then snarled: 'Logic is damn well not your *forté*, is it?'

She flinched in alarm, but when he made no move towards her she summoned energy sufficient to turn on him a look to indicate impatience with his obstinacy. 'There's no one else,' she repeated. 'That's logic enough for me. No one else it could've been.' She gave him a grim half smile she meant for triumph.

In response, he shot from his bench, tugged her to her feet, held her at arm's length. She gave a yelp of fright. 'Listen to me,' he said, controlling his voice now, his eyes on hers. 'You're talking rubbish. Pure, unmitigated rubbish. What you're saying doesn't make sense. You'd better think again and come up with something better. Whatever that damned tour guide told you, I'm not your man. I am *not* the "friend." I couldn't have been. I never laid eyes on you, didn't know of your existence, before you hailed me in the parking lot in Ephesus. Now, have you got that?' He relaxed his grip on her upper arms, let her go, turned, stalked back to the bench opposite.

She, too, sat, or rather collapsed. She found herself tempted to believe him. The inconsistencies that had occurred to her earlier crowded back into her mind.

"A boy gave the message to the guide,' came from Trevor, after a time.

'A boy, telling him to go off without me,' she now assisted. 'Telling him I'd met an old friend and that the friend had a car and would drive me, so I could rejoin the tour later on in Istanbul.'

'Quite a long message, a detailed one—and a *spoken* one?'

'Yes.'

'A boy,' he pursued. 'A boy you'd find at Ephesus, a village boy; selling postcards and what not, on the look-out for tourists around the parking lot, was asked to take this message—'

'I suppose so, yes.'

He rose and strode back and forth, slapping his hands to his sides as he spoke. 'Has it not occurred to you that this sort of boy, the only sort of urchin you'd find in a place like Ephesus, would understand only Turkish?—He could say in English "hello" and "please" and "you buy, very cheap" and "thank you very much"—*but he couldn't understand and convey the message you've described*! He bloody couldn't have! And what follows?'

'I don't know.'

'It follows that the type who gave the boy the message was a

Turk, every bit as much a Turk as your Kadir—because my Turkish is almost non-existent.'

Was Trevor lying? Did he really not speak Turkish? Was it certain that none of the Turkish boys haunting Ephesus knew English? Her head ached—the lateness of the hour, the wine, the raki. She couldn't think any more. She must resign herself to temporary retreat, to letting matters rest.

However, he would not. 'It was probably an admirer, that "friend"—one of those hot-blooded Turks,' he now taunted.

'He knew my name,' she said wearily. 'Knew my name, used it.'

Trevor considered this. 'Overheard it, maybe? Yes, an admirer, a hot-blooded Turk, set on a conquest, but then I came blundering along instead. Remember what the old boar hunters said about Turkish men?'—He sighed, suddenly unwilling to give more thought to it. Her problem, after all. He looked at his watch. 'Now where's that damned train?—You know what? Hasan must have forgotten it's Sunday!'

She felt miserable, marooned with him here. Her mouth was dry from the raki and wine. But of course the water here wouldn't be fit to drink. One thought recurred: whatever her present companion was or was not, whatever part he had or had not played in her affairs, she would be better off now, far far better off, if she had never made that decision to stay over yesterday in Selçuk. Bitterly, did she regret it; willingly did she thrust from her mind her former satisfaction in its having been her decision, rather a courageous one, and a sign of self-assertion, of renewal, of change. On this hard wooden bench in this chilly station waiting room—far worse, far more Spartan, than the room at Croesus—she must pass the remainder of the night. Wretched prospect!

'By the way,' he broke in after a long silence between them, 'I told you that something odd happened. The oddest thing, when I was coming back after collecting my stuff from the hotel.'

She didn't want to hear. 'Not now, I can't—'

Ignoring this, he rose once more, came to stand staring down fixedly at her. 'That fellow in the Mercedes, the one I call M—I assumed he'd stayed parked in the side street but he'd taken to circling the hotel instead; and on my way back from the hotel, when I'd worked my way down the road far enough to cross without being seen from the side street, he came along. They dip their headlights in towns; M turned his up just as I was crossing, full on me.'

'So?'

'He could've accelerated and run me down!'

'*Run you down*?—Why would he do that?'

'I told you—'

'In revenge for the bloody nose you gave his pal?'

'Forget the bloody nose. It was a bit worse.'

'Worse? Bad enough to run you down?'

'Definitely.'

'So you're changing your story, now.'

He continued undeterred: 'I waited behind a closed-up newspaper kiosk. He came by again, stopped opposite the hotel, and reversed into that same side street beside the *locanta*—to wait and watch, as before. It doesn't make sense: his being there means he connects me with what happened, yet he's not interested in running me down.'

'Maybe, in the dark, he didn't recognise you.'

'He had me, bang in his headlights, metres away—'

She heaved a long sigh. 'Well, you have nothing to worry about, then, have you? There's no grudge, no plot for bloody vengeance for the bloody nose or whatever it was. You ought to be pleased. Now you can forget the whole thing.' She'd gone far enough with him in this incomprehensible conversation. She would go no further. She must get her feet up. 'I'm going to flake out on this bench,' she said. 'I've been sitting, in the restaurant, in a van and here, for close on six hours.' She swung her legs up on the bench, wrapped her raincoat around them, and wedged her shoulder bag under her head for a pillow. Sleep was out of the question; she would merely rest and listen and be ready to spring up at the first sound of a ticket collector or a train. She closed her eyes. No sound disturbed her except, periodically, the tap of her companion's restless steps—marking his return to the main door, from which he peered as though for reassurance (or the pretence of it, she suspected) that no one had followed him here.

An hour passed, then two. Trevor lay stretched out, rigid and uncomfortable, on the bench opposite her, flat on his back with his arms folded across his chest. He listened for the car that Hasan had mentioned, and for the whistle of an approaching locomotive. At length he sensed the stealthy lifting of darkness, heard the first tentative twittering of birds. His thoughts kept returning to the question of M's inaction. What was meant by it? That he had arranged to deal with him differently, in some better place and by some surer method? But what could have been better than the dark deserted street, what surer than tramping on the accelerator of the Mercedes just then? Was he to conclude that M really didn't know what he looked like; that he hadn't, after all, closely observed him when they'd passed each other on the slopes of Mount Pion? Yet somehow M had tracked him to the Croesus. And there was no one else to confuse him with. He was the hotel's only guest—apart from Carey.

He saw her sitting in the straight-backed chair in his room at the Croesus, starting tentatively on the picnic, asking him what *ekmek* was. The picture, following on his thoughts of M, brought the two of them into peculiar conjunction. Just about the time M had been quitting the parking lot for the path up Mount Pion she would have been at the far end of it getting into a state about her bus; and a little earlier she would have been down below the Theatre, loitering near the Library of Celsus, or strolling up the Street of the Merchants—down below the Theatre, just when he, Trevor, was at the top of it, fighting off the man with the rifle. Had it not been for him she might have caught a stray bullet. He saw her as she had been next day, climbing the steps of the Theatre; saw the startled look on her face when he had greeted her unexpectedly, caught her, prevented her from slipping.—And now she wanted only to be rid of him. This was surely not cause for regret. Yet it hurt his pride. Women usually fell all over him—Suzanne among them. Which was why he'd promised himself a change. He hated himself for having swerved from his idea of an *affaire à la turque*, for not waiting for something in Istanbul or Izmir, the sister of one of his colleagues at Aphrodisias, whose phone number he'd been given, or a university student wanting to learn English, or even some *odalisque*, working the bar of an American hotel—ideally, resembling as closely as possible one of those superbly breasted and buttocked beauties in Ingre's painting, *Le Bain Turc*. Eastern, exotic, different. Above all, different.

His thoughts returned to Carey's having been at the hotel. Was there some peculiar significance attaching to the fact, demanding to be looked at more closely? What was it? He'd been thinking of M and of the man he'd killed, then of Carey. All three of them, one after another.

Then it came to him: an idea which caused him to get up and take several agitated turns about the room. Was it possible, he now asked himself, that M's interest centred on *her* rather than on himself? And therefore that the preparations of the man with the rifle at Ephesus had been made with her in mind, also?

Shaking his head and mumbling to himself that the idea was preposterous, he went outside once more to stare up and down the tracks. He tried to dismiss it from his mind, this preposterous idea; but he soon found he could not. Carey had been in not just one, but two, of the right places at the right time: somewhere below the Theatre at Ephesus when the man was above, and booked in at the hotel when M was on the prowl. The idea also took care of the latter's indifference towards Trevor in the street in Selçuk. Trembling with the chill of the night and his own speculation, he re-entered the waiting room and resumed his place at a distance opposite her. She lay on her side, turned from him, not moving, but he guessed not asleep.

A daft idea? Surely it was. Yet he knew so little about her, almost nothing. He'd told her how hard he thought it was really knowing someone. Maybe she had enemies. Or else it was a case of mistaken identity. He quite admitted he didn't want anything untoward happening to her. He cared to that extent. Warning her would mean recounting what happened up in the Theatre at Ephesus, telling her everything. He saw that at once. How would she take this newest twist, finding herself in the company of a killer?

Before he could answer himself, Carey sat up and eased her legs from the bench. The toilets, of the primitive, foot-marked, hole-in-the-floor variety, were off to the far side of the room. She made for them, feeling slightly dizzy, without uttering a word to him.
He waited tensely until she reappeared. 'Didn't sleep?'

'Of course not,' she snapped back.

He had returned from another glance into the street, having decided not to say anything to her. No, the whole idea was ridiculous.—Still, he could not convince himself of this, could not stop the idea nagging him; and, raising his eyes to hers now as she neared him, he abruptly changed his mind.

'There's something I'd better tell you,' he brought out. 'Something that may be important… . But you won't like it.'

God, what now? she wondered.

'Important for you, I mean. Then again, maybe not. I hope it isn't.'

'Don't bother. It couldn't be important. The only thing that could possibly be important would be the arrival of the damn train.'

He approached and stood looking down at her. 'There was ... an accident, up in that Theatre at Ephesus. I was attacked by someone.'

She sat looking wearily back at him. 'You told me.'

'This man tried to kill me—'

'*Kill* you!' She tipped her head and frowned sceptically.

'*Would* have killed me. He went for my throat like a bloody pit bull.'

'With his teeth, I suppose—'

'Dammit, I'm not just telling you this to get it off my chest! The fact is, he didn't succeed; he didn't kill me.'

'Obviously—'

'No.' He paused until she met his gaze. '*I* killed *him*!' He fell briefly silent, content to let the point sink in.

'I ... don't believe you.' There was a tremor in her voice.

He produced a grim smile. 'Well, you'd better. Because it's the truth. I killed the fellow. Not that I meant to. It was in self-defence. But I did kill him. I left him dead as a mackerel.'

She raised her hand to her throat, as if to protect it.

'In self-defence,' he repeated. 'But Carey, why I'm telling you this is—'

'Yes, why are you telling me this?' she cried. 'I don't want to know! I don't! Just shut up about it and leave me alone!' She fully believed him. It was perfectly true. He had killed someone. But it wasn't enough. He got a perverse thrill out of telling someone, dwelling on what he'd done. And now that he'd told her, confided this to her, he couldn't let her live, could he? No, he couldn't! He would kill her next!

'Carey, get hold of yourself.' He squatted down and tried unsuccessfully to take her hand. 'Why I'm telling you this,' he resumed determinedly, 'is that this fellow had a rifle and seemed to be preparing to shoot someone down below in the town.—Are you listening?—He was preparing to shoot someone down below. Or that's how it looked.'

Trevor got no further. A sound cut in, a sound that caused Carey to snatch up her shoulder bag and scramble for the door, leaving Trevor to retrieve and struggle into his backpack. The locomotive slipped past in clouds of steam, and came to a halt. There were only two carriages and apparently no conductor, no other passengers. The whistle blew and the carriages briefly slid backwards with the releasing of the brakes, even as Trevor appeared beside her.

'Here,' he shouted, opening the door of an empty compartment and helping her up.

Once inside, she bit his hand, fought him—tried savagely to prevent his joining her, to shut and lock the door against him, as the locomotive wrenched its burden forward, as though to aid her in shaking him off.

But it was not to be. Gathering momentum, going on its charted way, the train seemed to sigh and groan in recognition of failure—as, panting, he clawed his way in and dropped down beside her.

## Chapter 10

'As I SAID, it happened in the Theatre at Ephesus,' he continued tensely, when he saw she had stopped crying. 'Just before you and I met, as a matter of fact—just before you called out to me down in the parking lot.'

The colour had drained from her face. She seemed not to hear.

'Carey?—You're shaking; do you want my coat?'

'No!' She shrank from him.

'It was at the very top,' he pressed on. 'At the top, where you and I were yesterday morning—where the rows of seats end and there's a wall, made by slabs of stone leaning into the hillside. That's why I went back.'

'Not for me.'

'No.'

'You lied.'

'Yes. That time, yes.'

She could do nothing. She was alone with a murderer, alone with him in the compartment, a bare wooden interior, a cubicle with blackened brass fittings and cigarette-burned sills. Her frenzied glance rose to the emergency chain.

'No!' he shot out, gripping her wrists, so that she cried out in pain. 'Don't pull it! Not until I've finished telling you.—Then you can, if you still want to.' One of his hands turned her face, forcing her to look at him. 'All right? I promise you can, but only after I've finished telling you what I have to tell you.' He made her nod, in his hand.

'I was sitting on my jacket doing a rough sketch, a sort of plan of part of the town, when this man arrived.' He flung himself opposite her, hopeful of having her meet his gaze. She sat, miserably counseling herself not to annoy him, but to try to listen, to humour him, as he began his story: how he had been perched up there, making a sketch of the foundations visible along the Street of the Merchants; how he had taken out his Swiss knife and opened the main blade to sharpen his *conté* pencil, how one moment he'd been alone and the next this individual had materialized, standing with his back to him—a couple of legs in black trousers and the backside of a mac with a piece of the lining torn and hanging down. 'Are you listening?'

'I'm … trying.'

Unsure, he repeated what he had said. 'He hadn't seen me,' he continued, more composedly now. 'I was miffed, felt he'd invaded my privacy. I mean, he had the whole damned Theatre. I tried like hell to remember what "Good afternoon" is in Turkish but all I could come up with was '*Gunaydin*'—Good Morning—not quite the ticket for late afternoon. Meanwhile, this fellow was putting together bits and pieces he'd had strapped under his coat and in his pockets. In my innocence I thought of a camera tripod or surveyor's equipment, but then I saw he'd turned the bits and pieces into a rifle—aye, a rifle. The butt was a light metal frame. Like in *The Day of the Jackal*—remember?'

She shook her head. She hadn't seen the film.

'The thing had telescopic sights and a piece along the end of the barrel, a cylinder, which must've been a silencer.'

She frowned, making an effort now to follow, trying to picture the seated and the standing figure, the assembling of the rifle.

'A sort of embarrassment hit me—mingled, of course, with fear. The self-preservation instinct. I was about to witness a murder (rightly or wrongly, that's what sprang to mind)—as good as dead myself, in other words. The adrenaline pumps kicked in and my brain cells all lit up at once. I watched him snugging himself against his stone and looking like he was about to sight the rifle. I wasn't near enough that back path he'd come up; and descending the nearest aisle of the Theatre in the conventional way meant leaving my backside exposed to this fellow and his rifle. I was trapped, so I thought I'd better say something—before whatever was going to happen happened. It seemed better than afterwards. I didn't want to be a witness. I struggled to my feet and blurted "*Merhaba*!"

'"Merhaba"?'

'It means hello.'

'And then—?' She was with him tentatively now. She couldn't help herself.

'He turned manic, spun around as though he'd been goosed, flung down his weapon and went for my throat. His fingers closed on my windpipe and I couldn't breathe. I was blacking out. I knew I only had a few seconds to do something, if I wanted to stay alive. And as it happened I still had the Swiss knife in my hand. I slashed and prodded—blind. I didn't want to kill him. Naturally, I didn't want to kill him. All I wanted was to get him off me.'

'But you did, you really did … kill him.'

He nodded, drew breath. 'In flailing out like that I happened to slash the bugger's throat.'

His throat. Her own felt suddenly dry as sandpaper. Could he be fabricating all this, for some reason? In spite of herself, she began to think not. 'Self-defence—'

'I remember swaying on my knees, crawling with head down so things would come back into focus; trying to balance, feel my neck—with my head drooped near tufts of grass and the occasional daisy. Blood was still spurting from him. Funny, I was concerned about the pencil!—It was *conté*, quite expensive. I remember picking it up, seeing it hadn't snapped. Can you imagine? Then I noticed the edges of my sketchbook—on the ground, half under him, soaking up blood; so I staggered up and wiped the pages and shoved the sketchbook back into the bag I'd brought it in—maybe trying to behave as if nothing had happened. I asked myself why I couldn't have just nicked him, made him give up his grip.—This,' he added with a burst of false jocularity, 'is the murder weapon. You wouldn't think the blade long enough to do much damage.'

At the sight of the knife she flinched. On his pocketing it again, she looked at him searchingly. 'The blood—there would have been a lot of it. On you, too.'

He nodded. 'On the ground and between the stones. Some on my shirt and hands. I wiped my hands on the grass, hid the shirt under my jacket when I put it back on.'

Her mind sped to and fro over what he had described. Hard to believe in a man with a rifle, a struggle, a killing, and when she'd visited the very spot herself and noticed nothing in particular. Yet it made sense of so much: his surliness on their walk, his watching at the window in his room that night, his apparently painful neck, the stained tee-shirt and sketchbook.

'I thought I'd better tell you,' he said.

'The rifle—?'

'I left it. I didn't touch it.'

'And the body?'

'Maybe his chum, who was on his way up the path when I passed him. I assume it was his chum—from the Mercedes. Or else the police. He didn't just get up and walk away on his own.—Although that's just what the police in Selçuk seemed to want to make me think.'

'You went to the police? You told them?'—She felt a surge of something like relief. This added dimension of authority seemed to make his story more credible, and him slightly less frightening.

'This morning—well, yesterday morning now, just before I saw you on top of the Theatre. But they didn't have much to say. In fact they were useless. At first they seemed to think I'd invented the whole thing; then they appeared to want to reassure me I hadn't hurt the fellow fatally and that he'd made off on his own. In the end they actually suggested I forget about the whole affair.'

'But why?'

'I don't know. I told them I had no intention of leaving it like that.'

'But—'

'They were the Tourist Police and they're onto tourism to solve the country's problems. It's just possible they didn't want it bruted abroad that people can get murdered at one of the country's prime tourist attractions. Bad for business.'

'That seems—'

'Far-fetched?—I don't know.'

'Who was he?'

Trevor sighed, and shook his head. 'I should've gone through the bugger's pockets but I couldn't bring myself to touch him, and after looking around and being pretty sure no one had seen anything all I could think of was getting the hell out of there.'

'A Turk?'

'I'd say so. A big fellow, lots of flesh on him—and I daresay muscle; crop of black hair, moustache, bad teeth. I assumed—I guess I still do—that he was a terrorist of some stripe or other. According to Hasan, the military haven't managed to crack down on all of them. Then again, he just might have been something else entirely—'

'Like what?'

'Well, *inside* the law. Just there to protect someone special. Maybe I misread the whole scenario. Maybe he wouldn't have actually fired at anyone.'

'But would he have attacked you, then?'

'Depends who he thought I was.'

A silence followed, during which she thought over what he had told her, and he shifted uncomfortably with the knowledge that there was more to come. You're stalling, you bastard, he told himself. Get on with it. Tell her. She'll say I'm daft and it'll be a relief if she can persuade me I am, a hell of a relief. He had, in telling her about the incident in the Theatre, imperceptibly warmed towards her. 'But Carey,' he resumed hesitantly, 'I had this idea—'

She was busily, tensely, thinking: Why am I siding with him, even a little? If he really has killed this person, then doesn't that make him just that much worse, put him beyond the pale, in fact? Why should I believe he couldn't have knocked the man out, done something less than kill him?

'Carey?'

'What?'

'I told you all this for a reason. It wasn't just to get it off my chest.'

She nodded absently.

'Carey, you've got to listen. Please. I had this idea, this—maybe crazy—idea.'

Spare me, she said beneath her breath. No more, please. I don't want to get involved. I just don't want to get involved. Whatever it is. Leave me out of it.

'I've got to tell you because only you can deal with it.'

'Please, no—' she murmured wearily.

'I said I'd been seen by the fellow in Selçuk, "M", in the Mercedes, and that he looked right through me, didn't try to run me over, showed not the slightest interest, and that I couldn't understand it. Well then, let's suppose *I'm* not the one he's after … . Suppose he hasn't connected me with what happened to his chum, and that the payoff for the job he's been assigned is enough of an incentive for him to simply get on with it.'

She nodded.

'Suppose he hasn't any alternative.'

She nodded once more.

'Now, assuming the job means eliminating someone, who could that be? Who are the candidates?'

'How should I know?'

'Well, just think about it.'

'I can't.'

'Think about it!'

'I can't!'

'You must!'

'I don't know enough about Turkey, about their quarrels,' she said irritably.

'Carey—'

She heaved a sigh. 'Maybe there was some Greek involved. Some agent. They said there may be a war. You aren't to know who or what he was. You'll never know.—Now, can't you leave it at that?'

'No, I'm not keen on spending the rest of my life in the dark about the whole business, my days poisoned by uncertainty, not even knowing whose side the man I killed belonged to. Besides—'

'Arabs,' she volunteered, remembering something. 'There was an Arab, in the Library of Celsus, coming by as I left it; an Arab in a headdress, with three women trailing after him all swaddled up and someone in a suit who might have been a chauffeur.'

He remembered them, too. 'Wives, or family—and a bodyguard.' But it was no good, no help at all.

Annoyed with herself for offering suggestions that seemed to turn her into an accomplice, she glared at the floor.

He was frowning darkly, shaking his head. 'The trouble is, targeting an Arab at Ephesus doesn't explain the interest M appeared to be taking in the Hotel Croesus when you and I were in the *locanta*. There wasn't an Arab staying at the Croesus … . There was only you and me.' He waited, but she remained silent. No point in holding back, he told himself. No point at all. 'Now listen carefully,' he said. 'Just listen, and then I'll shut up and you can tell me to go to hell. The point is, neither I nor your Arab was in both the right places … *but you were*, and at the right times!'

'*What*?'—Her eyes widened in astonishment.

'Think about it,' he persevered.

'What are you saying?'

'You were below the Theatre in Ephesus at about the time my man was assembling his rifle. The type I passed on the path came from the Mercedes, which was in the parking lot and then prowling around the Hotel Croesus, where *you* were staying in Selçuk.'

Her brain seemed to explode. He was mad, inexplicably mad; he was after all sadistic, determined to keep up the pressure, envenom the moment. He'd reverted to what he'd been at the beginning, on their walk to the bus stop in Selçuk. My first impression of him was right, she told herself. First impressions always are. I should never have had anything more to do with him.—The point of the whole story of his killing the man in the Theatre became instantly clear to her. She retorted, almost wildly, that this latest attempt to frighten her—for reasons best known to himself—his idea of *her* being the intended victim of anyone, was absurd. No one wished her dead. Was that clear? No one. She had no enemies. She had offended no one.

'Logic isn't your *forté*,' he commented dryly.

'Logic!—You call that logic? I tell you I have no enemies, not one!'

'Maybe you were mistaken for someone else,' he calmly rejoined.

Her voice shook. 'You've tried your best to frighten me with this, haven't you? Well, you haven't succeeded.' She stared at him fiercely. A tense silence fell between them; abruptly broken by her smiling a smile of triumph: 'Haven't you forgotten something?—*That I spent the whole of yesterday morning wandering about the ruins of Ephesus, alone mostly!*'

He registered surprise, then relief—tempered by the awareness that M's interest must centre on him after all. But it was true: anyone wanting to kill Carey would have had an ideal opportunity yesterday morning! He tried, unavailingly, to make her believe he was glad it was ridiculous.

Ridiculous. Yet he had, after all, notwithstanding her denial, succeeded in frightening her anew; and now, though relieved by her own fortuitous thought, she was left with an unpleasant feeling that the matter was not quite settled between them. She formed a picture of him striding ahead of her on the road between Selçuk and Ephesus, while the large black birds watched from their perches among the willows.

## Chapter 11

THE JOURNEY SEEMED agonizingly slow to her. Stops were made inexcusably, in hamlets at which no passengers appeared, and the station master or some other railway functionary seemed to be the only person out of bed. Beyond the soot-grimed window drifted a bland landscape of pallid green fields and low hills. At length she became aware of the panting effort of the locomotive, challenged by a steepening gradient; and she gazed out on a bleaker, more rugged, landscape of dark conifers and glistening rock-faces and fast-flowing, ochre-coloured rivulets.

She felt underslept, miserable, hopelessly confused. The wine, the raki, and now this bombshell, this absurd idea—hard on the news that her companion was a killer (if she was to believe him). She had left home and husband thinking, hoping, that against a background of new and stimulating surroundings she would see herself afresh. She had imagined, in taking her decision to stay over in Selçuk, that she might return with more to give, having vanquished her notion of inadequacy. Now, it seemed, she had slipped back, lost her bearings entirely. Here was no clarity, no advance. She had been three days in Turkey and all was confusion. She had become the plaything of mischievous and malefic forces, strange new gods; through Trevor, their agent or messenger. Recollections now appeared as omens, some fearful, all pointing to her present hapless state: the blood stains of dead mosquitoes decking the walls and ceiling of her room at Mr Deverli's hotel, the blood stains on Trevor's sketchbook and tee-shirt, the paper-bag picnic punctuated by the *muezzin*'s eerie chant; and Trevor's tales of Gyges's stabbing the king, of Croesus, of M and the yellow Mercedes in the *cul-de-sac*, which was not there. These took on harsh, jangling, surreal colours, as she brought them together in her mind like pieces tumbling in a kaleidoscope. There could be no truth in what he had suggested, no truth in his notion of someone intent on killing her. It was nonsense—obscurely, perversely, motivated. She was at present incapable of thinking clearly, logically, however. All she knew was that the idea had come from Trevor, and that she must more than ever regard him as someone dangerous to know.

Yet as the minutes passed and he continued to sit inoffensively and perfectly silent before her, she wanted desperately to learn what he was thinking.

In fact, he simply brooded on her infuriatingly mistaken opinion of him; and on his well-intended concern for her having made matters worse between them. Irreparably worse. They were farther apart than ever, the two of them, and now would remain so. Was it possible that he cared a little after all, or simply that he disliked the idea of failure? In any case he must resign himself: she would rejoin her flock and be herded to all the prescribed places. Perhaps she would think of him kindly when she reached Troy and saw it was as he'd said, just a few scattered stones and post-card kiosks. He looked across her at the passing rocks and trees and considered his own situation. *Her* being out of danger didn't mean *he* was. Yes, Carey's having wandered unharmed in Ephesus yesterday morning assuredly meant M's interest centered in him after all. He supposed he could hide himself well enough in Istanbul; yet would he feel truly safe, even after some time had passed, and he was back at work with his colleagues in Aphrodisias?

In the continuing silence Carey suddenly decided there would be no point in parting from him in outright hostility. She had recovered somewhat from her initial shock. Izmir and freedom were minutes away. She would be saying good-bye to him. She found herself calmer; and now she ventured so far as to wonder if his idea might after all have arisen from some genuine, if wildly wrongheaded, concern for her safety. He had done her no actual harm, after all. 'Izmir,' she inquired, 'is it famous for anything?'

'Nemesis,' he replied, still with his eyes on the landscape. 'And a massacre.'

'Nemesis—'

He turned and met her gaze. 'Daughter of Night and goddess of revenge.'

More blood and mayhem, she thought. Another omen, perhaps?

'The mountain we're just crossing was supposed to be her home. It slopes to the city and the sea.'

'I know about the massacre.'

'Yes, ending here, really, in 1921. The Greeks considered this part of the world theirs from away back. The Turks drove them and a lot of Armenians into the sea. The city burned for three days.'

Now that she felt herself almost on safe ground and about to part from Trevor for ever, she could find it in her heart to hope the goddess of revenge was not waiting for him in Izmir. She turned to the window as the train ran easily down amid the first houses and factories that announced the city of Nemesis and the massacre. It had rained hard all during the time she was here before. She had been tired then, taken in little; she was exhausted now, but at least it wasn't raining. She watched as the city spread itself upon the lower slopes, a display of terra cotta roofs and creamy plaster walls. The complacent and cheerful aspect clashed with the picture presented by history and myth. White appartment blocks and shining minarets stood against an innocent blue spring sky. Surely, nothing approaching a massacre could have taken place here. Yesterday, on an equally splendid morning, the site of the supposed killing at the Theatre in Ephesus had struck her as equally inappropriate. The streets as the train slowed became wide and spacious. Just as it pulled into Izmir's Basmane Gari she glimpsed the shining sea.

They hurried through the station and found a taxi. The clock suspended on the soot-soaked architrave of the station entrance showed 8.10.

'The tour bus may not leave until 8.30,' she said breathlessly. 'I could just make it.'

'I don't normally take taxis,' he grumbled. 'I hate them almost as much as I hate flying.'

The taxi sped along wide uncrowded avenues then turned to follow the shoreline.

'Pretty inconvenient for you, I guess—if you hate taxis and flying,' she said to put in time.

'Taxis drive like hell—especially Turkish ones.'

'And flying?'

'I once almost caught a plane that was blown up by someone keen on cashing his wife's insurance policy.'

She saw the hotel's sign only a couple of blocks ahead. She burrowed in her shoulder bag for her wallet and portioned off a small wad of liras. 'On me,' she said, giving them to him. 'Do you realise no one asked us to buy a ticket for the train? We had a free ride.' She had now little money but could get more at the hotel. 'You'll take the taxi on, then?'

'I won't take a taxi any further than I can help,' came the churlish reply. 'Besides, I like walking by the sea.'

The taxi halted. They got out. She extended her hand to him, but he refused to take it. 'You have a way of missing busses. Wouldn't you like me to wait, in case you've missed this one too?'

She swung her bag towards a blue bus that had halted beyond the hotel entrance. His expression soured. 'Aegean Sun Fun Tours,' he read out from its side.

'Good-bye, Trevor.'—She turned quickly and fled up the hotel steps.

Gleaming marble, vividly coloured rugs and hangings, columns graciously fluted and scrolled, liveried lackies scurrying and attending—all these made an immediate and favourable impression on Carey Signorello as she entered the grand foyer of the hotel. Her world, she told herself. Things would be better now. Her world, after all. Far removed from the squalid little front room of the Croesus, with its broken-springed chair and equally run-down occupant! And no mosquitoes left squashed on the walls of any of the palatial rooms above!

Her world, yet a feeling crept over her that she could no longer take her own place in it for granted. She found herself re-entering with a certain dismay. It was as though she had been swept into a familiar room full of her own guests and forgotten all their names, or begun to suspect in the midst of one of her husband's business parties that she had lost one of her earrings.

A picture of Trevor intervened: she saw him walking away from her, alone, beside the sea, and wanted obscurely to say something more to him.

Shielded by the cascading leaves and blossoms of an immense oleander from most of the occupants of the foyer, she looked into the marble distance and immediately recognised several members of the Aegean Sun Fun tour, huddled together with coats and cameras on their arms. People from home. The next instant her eyes came to rest on the ample backside of Gloria Bloomquist. Gloria had stooped to right a small green case which had lost a wheel. Now she was towing it lopsidedly to join other cases that had already been collected at the far end of the room. Beyond the cases a pair of tall glass doors led through to the waiting bus.

Gloria, and people from home. All looking like what they were: tourists, Americans, mostly middle-aged, ordinary. Unable to disguise themselves and feeling no necessity to do so, unable to change—but why should they? For some reason she felt momentarily disinclined to be one of them. Kadir had now arrived and was addressing them briefly. They were filing out. By the glass doors the suitcases were being loaded by two porters onto a wagon. Among them Carey thought she glimpsed her own.

She stood irresolute a moment or two longer, before reminding herself she needed money.

At the desk the librarian-like receptionist smiled perfunctorily but then stood frowning and sucking on the tortoise-shell patterned frame of her glasses as Carey explained that her passport was in her suitcase. 'With that bunch over there,' she said—only to see through the front windows that the wagon had already trundled out and that suitcases were being loaded into the freight compartment of the bus.

'You should keep you passport with you, Mrs Signorello,' scolded the receptionist.

'I know, I know—'

'I'm very sorry—'

'But I *stayed* here!—And my bus is leaving any minute!—Surely you can change the travellers' cheque without—'

'But you see, Mrs Signorello, I require the number.'

She would have to dash for the suitcase, hoping the side pocket with the passport hadn't been buried under other cases by the time she got to it. Turning, she found her way blocked by one of the youngest of the hotel's liveried lackies. 'Mrs Signorello?'

'Yes? What is it? I'm in a hurry—'

'Excuse me, but a gentleman was here for you, Madam.'

'Gentleman?'

'Yes, Madam.'

Gentleman? For her? There was some mistake. Yet she paled with a sense of foreboding.

'Yesterday afternoon. Asking for you. I thought you like to know.'

It was as though she had been walking confidently barefoot in her garden and stepped on a slug. Trevor couldn't have been here in Izmir. Not yesterday afternoon.

'Your friend,' rejoined the boy, frowning now, less sure of himself, or his tip.

Friend?—Again, that word. *But not Trevor*. No possibility of it's being Trevor. Not this time.—Dreading something, without the least understanding of what it might be, she struggled to keep her voice calm. She must not frighten the boy; he had still to explain. She felt a desperate need to make sense of this. 'Ah, I see.' She nodded, managed to smile.

'He take me aside, ask me for you,' he went on, encouraged. 'He spend a long time just waiting, before. I noticed him in the lobby. When the bus return and you not with it, he come to ask for you. He left no message but I think you like to know.'

'Asked for me by name?'

'Yes, Madam—by name.'

'And what else? What did he want?'

'Just why you are not here, where you are, when you come back, where you going next.'

Carey's brain spun, her pulses raced. 'And what did you tell him?' she asked, making a huge effort to hold the walnut eyes of the boy as if to make him an accomplice in mischief. 'And what did you tell him?' she repeated. 'I hope you gave him some information, did you?'

'Oh yes, but I could not assist him very much, you see, because I did not know—'

'But you told him something, I hope?'

'Only that you stay in Selçuk, and join the others later on in Istanbul. I remember that you stay at the Hilton Hotel in Istanbul because I hear Kadir make a joke with one of the porters, that you have met someone nicer than him but he will see you back in Istanbul because he have your suitcase.'

'Ah, good. You mentioned all that, too—Istanbul, the suitcase, the Hilton?'

'Yes, Madam.'

'Good. And what did he look like?'

The boy stood mute, surprised by the question.

'I ... just want to be sure he was my friend,' she said with a laugh. 'Are you good at describing people?'

'He was ... big.' The boy spread his arms. 'Bald, also.' He grinned.

Her voice quavered as she thanked him. Her fingers trembled as she dug from her bag a five-hundred lira note for him.

So Trevor had not lied!—I've been getting everything wrong, she told herself miserably. But I don't understand! I just don't! Oh Trevor, now I'm never going to be able to find you!—He had become important to her, so very important, to an extent unimaginable just moments before. Retreating behind the oleander she recalled what Mario had let slip on his return from that business trip to Turkey last year, about making enemies and not being in a hurry to go back there. Did what was happening have anything to do with those same enemies? She could give no thought to that now; she must decide what to do. All she knew was that she couldn't rejoin the tour, couldn't possibly be where she had arranged to be. Her eyes travelled to the big blue bus throbbing beyond the tall glass doors on the far side of the foyer and stayed fixed on it until it pulled away and was replaced by a lilac coloured taxi.

Several more minutes passed before she was able to convince herself that by stepping forward and exposing herself to general view beyond the oleander she would not be risking her life. Who else could the friend be but Trevor's man, M? But *why*? Who was he? She could be thankful he wasn't here now. Yesterday afternoon he'd been told she would not adhere to the tour's itinerary but return to the Izmir Palas. Also that she would not reappear until the Hilton in Istanbul. If only she had told Trevor to wait! If only—! Ten long minutes ago she had turned her back on him voluntarily, thankfully, telling herself she wanted nothing more to do with him. She saw the esplanade, curving around the bay in a blaze of sunlight and lapping water. He had strode off. Where, she did not know.

The picture of him, distancing himself further from her with every second, brought her close to panic. She put on her dark glasses and stepped clear of the oleander. Keeping to the wall, trying not to hurry, she worked her way to the main entrance of the hotel.—She heard herself descending the steps, the heels of her shoes striking the stone and echoing from the tall roof of the *porte cochère*. She hurried now, threading her way through the formal gardens fronting the hotel, crossing the coastal road to the wide palm-lined esplanade.

'Taxi, Madam?'—The lilac coloured taxi had given up on the hotel and now crawled beside her at the curb.

Trevor was nowhere in sight. She quickened her pace, while the taxi kept even with her.

'Taxi?'—the driver was grinning aside at her. 'I speak English. My English good.'

She halted in despair. 'Yes, all right,' she heard herself say. 'Yes.' She got in. 'I want to find someone, by the sea.'—But which way?

They drove for a time, first one way alongside the esplanade, then the other. She sat perched on the back seat, clutching the sides of the seat in front, searching to left and right. He was nowhere to be seen. She told the driver to turn down one and then another of the narrow refuse-choked streets leading from the coastal road to the mayhem of small shops and day hotels; before deciding it was hopeless.

She looked back, also, but saw no yellow Mercedes. In the taxi she felt safe, but she could not very well stay in it. Where should she go?—'The bus station,' she called out, then changed her mind. 'No, the Tourist Police.' Trevor had said they speak English. 'The Tourist Police—are they far?'

'No far.'

'Good. And when we get there I want you to wait for me.'

## Chapter 12

BENEATH THE DAUNTLESS eyes of the regulation portrait of Ataturk and a sluggishly—and quite unnecessarily—revolving ceiling fan, she told her story to two members of the Tourist Police; saying in conclusion that she had refused to believe anyone would want to kill her, but had then remembered her husband's having made enemies on his last trip here, and that there had been threats against his life. These enemies now sought to take revenge on him by killing her. Had it not been for the accidental intervention of a stranger, a Scottish archaeologist, a Mr Trevor Malcolm, one of these people would have succeeded in doing away with her at Ephesus. The other had searched for her yesterday at the Izmir Palas, then returned to Selçuk and only just missed her there. He would be waiting when she arrived at the Hilton Hotel in Istanbul.

'You imagine your husband's enemies would think themselves revenged on him by killing you?' inquired the elder of the two policemen, frowning.

'It's the only explanation.'

'With such enemies, why did your husband allow you to come here?'

She defended Mario. Some months had passed since his visit here; a continuance of the animosity, its relevance to her, would never have occurred to him. The policeman, suffering from a cold, nodded, then sneezed. The younger man sat deferentially to one side, stroking his chin and looking thoughtful.

The ensuing silence was punctuated by the ringing of the telephone and an interlude of Turkish.

'Our colleagues in Selçuk,' the elder man explained, apparently brought more to life by the exchange. He blew his nose, then looked up from his handkerchief, intent on assessing Carey's reaction to what he was about to say. 'Mrs Signorello, the woman I spoke to just now can find no record of any interview with a Mr Malcolm.'

'No record—?'

He slowly shook his head. 'Nothing.'

'But—'

'And as to the, rather sensational, event you have described as having taken place in the Theatre at Ephesus ... there appears to be no record of that either.'

'But there must be!'

'Apparently not.'

'But there was a dead man—!'

'A body was not found.'

'The other man took it, then. That's what must have happened. My friend, Mr Malcolm, saw him going up the path in back of the Theatre.'

'That may be. -How long have you known this Mr Malcolm?'

'Not ... very long. Three days.'

'Ah.'

The older man exchanged glances with his younger colleague, who then proceeded to make polite requests for her to go over this or that. Carey saw that the phone call had robbed her of credibility. Hardest for these men to accept was the incident at Ephesus itself, the accidental killing—at the hands of an archaeologist wielding a Swiss knife. Admirable as a Swiss knife was in its way, the younger man remarked, its uses could hardly be imagined to extend much beyond wood carving, opening tins and bottles, or clipping and filing fingernails. If only the body had not gone mysteriously missing things would be so much simpler. The body and the records with the Selçuk police.

'Mrs Signorello,' the older man offered at length, after blowing his nose once more and this time carefully inspecting his sodden handkerchief, 'you claim your life is in danger. We are not convinced of this, as you see. I am sure you do not understand Turkey. Our ways are different. Our men are ... forward. A woman like yourself, a western woman—young, and, permit me to say, beautiful—is unusual here in Turkey and may attract a particular man, who will follow her, not necessarily with evil intent. There need be no harm in this. Is it not possible that the person who inquired after you at the Izmir Palas yesterday afternoon was such man?'

And the killing in the Theatre?—You just don't believe it happened, do you?'

'As to the incident at Ephesus, it is difficult to decide, is it not? I am quite sure you are convinced it occurred. I do not question your sincerity, Mrs Signorello. Please do not think that. The incident may indeed have occurred. But let us not forget that we have only Mr Malcolm to trust on the matter—his story, and you have already disclosed that three days ago you did not know of his existence. Perhaps you underestimate yourself, Mrs Signorello. I put it to you that Mr Malcolm is as likely to have fallen under you charm as any other man. And therefore is it not possible that this was a bold invention on the part of your very new friend, in order to present himself to you in a favourable, a dramatic, light?'

Carey showed her annoyance by getting up without a word. The other rose also, from behind his desk, and raised his hand. 'Mrs Signorello, what is it exactly you expect us to do?'

'I never dreamed you wouldn't believe me. I just never thought that. I came here assuming you'd help me.'

'Yes, yes. But how?'

'By finding this man. By stopping him!'

'You mean, by arresting him? Assuming we could find him. Arresting him—but for what? The difficulty is that, so far as we know, he has committed no crime.'

'By giving me protection, then. Until I can retrieve my passport and get myself out of the country.'

The other pinched his nose to stop himself from sneezing.

'I could—,' the younger man interposed.

'Could what, Amil?'

Drive the lady to the airport, at least—for example.'

'Yes, of course!' he laughed, then coughed. 'And you would not mind the task, Amil. Not at all!—You see, Mrs Signorello, you have yet another admirer.' He shook his head and was about to add something in the same vein, but observing her close to tears of frustration and rage, chose to speak seriously and in a more kindly tone: 'Mrs Signorello, you say yourself that this man now knows about Istanbul—your going there, staying at the Hilton Hotel. You say the danger lies there. Quite rightly, one must assume. There, and not here. That is the point. This individual is perhaps not a killer—no, no, I really don't think he is. He may be simply a nuisance. But whatever he is he was given information which prompted him to leave Izmir. He was not at the Izmir Palas just now. Very well.' He raised his arms. 'Your are safe for now. Safe here. Do you agree?'

'Yes, I suppose so.'

'It is logical.'

She nodded.

'You saw no one.'

'That's true.'

'Very well. Then let us deal with the next step. Permit me to suggest that you simply take a bus to Istanbul. Once there you must stay at another hotel, obviously. You can have your suitcase sent for. It is very simple. Istanbul is large. You cannot possibly be found there if you do not wish to be. And the moment you receive your suitcase, with the passport, you can leave the country. I do not see any danger for you in this.'

Doubtless the advice was kindly meant and not unreasonable, yet she found it galling that neither of these men fully believed her. She judged further effort futile.

'My young colleague here will drive you to the bus station. Indeed, I believe he is eager to do so.'

Carey's defiance took them both by surprise. 'Thank you but I've kept my taxi.'

In the wake of this frustrating encounter with the Tourist Police she regretted more keenly than ever the departure of Trevor. Would he have boarded a bus, an hour or so ago? She told the taxi driver to take her to the bus station. Moments later, remembering how little money she now had left, she inquired: 'A bus to Istanbul, is it cheap?'

'Oh, yes.'

'And the bus station, is it near where you picked me up—near the Izmir Palas?'

The driver shook his head. 'Far from there,' he said. 'Other side of town.'

'There's no other way?' she thought of asking. 'No other way to get to Istanbul?'

'Ship.'

'Ship?'

'Overnight to Istanbul. She leave late afternoon. Next morning you are in the Sea of Marmara. Beautiful!'

The words brought to mind Trevor walking away from her—*beside the sea*. 'A ship—but where? Where do you get on?'

'Near Izmir Palas, where we started from!' He laughed. 'Just along the esplanade. Turkish Maritime Line. Not expensive.'

She leant forward, gripping the seat-back in front. He hates taxis; maybe he hates buses, too. And he went off along the esplanade! 'The ship is not expensive? Really not expensive?'

'Subsidized by government. For tourism.'

'I'm sorry, sorry to be changing my mind—but take me there, to that ship. Not the bus station, after all. And go as fast as you like. I mustn't miss it. I must get on that ship!'

'No problem. And no hurry—lots of time. Afternoon.'

Lots of time, afternoon—meaning there *was* a problem. 'How can I put in time till the ship leaves?—I'm dead tired. I don't want to walk around Izmir. I don't want to do anything like that. But I must put in time.' And stay out of sight, she silently added.

He thought for a minute, while humming an old Beatles song to assist the process. 'You like Turkish bath?'

'I've never—'

'I take you to buy ship ticket, then I drive you to public bath for women. You can stay there long time. No problem.' With a rapid glance over his shoulder he executed what seemed to Carey the most reckless of U-turns and accelerated in the direction from which they had come. 'A woman's privilege,' he laughed. 'To change her mind!'

## Chapter 13

A MAUVE HAZE hung over the city, between the twin-peaked mountain and the sea. At Pier J of the new Yeni Liman building at Alsançak Point the last passengers hastened with their bags and string-bound boxes up the gangway of the *M.V. Izmir*. A porter with a crate strapped to his back laboured after them, bent at a right angle to face his footsteps and the oily black water that coursed between the timbers of the quay and the rust-streaked flanks of the ship. Overhead the long tubular arms of a crane flailed in slow motion like the limbs of a giant upturned insect, manoeuvering, adjusting, so that a bright orange Peugeot 504 could be lowered into the remaining space on the main deck, where deckhands readied themselves to secure lines and fit chocs to it. Muzak blared throughout the ship. In the lounges the air was already thick with tobacco smoke. Along corridors stewards led first Class passengers to their cabins. Certain passengers were getting their bearings, exploring, trying locked doors, calling to one another with each fresh discovery, setting out across the newly swabbed decks as far forward as permitted and as far astern. Children peered down ventilators, climbed excitedly to the boat deck, hastened to the rails when a tug steamed past and hooted. Above the black striped funnel and the criss-crossing cables and the slanted arms of the cranes, gulls with black heads and black-tipped wings swooped and screamed.

Presently the Muzak ceased. An order crackled over the public address system from the bridge. Answering cries rose from the quay. The ship's decks and railings began to vibrate. A blast issued from her whistle, startling those not expecting it. The aquamarine sky heaved and undulated through thickened fumes sent from the high striped funnel. The gangway swung away; the lines sailed free, splashed and were hauled in. Gradually the ship slid sideways, backed, slowly swung round. The waters boiled in fury at her screws as she laboured towards the harbour mouth and the open sea. Astern, Ataturk Caddesi lengthened and seemed to spread itself like a trickle of honey, following in a gentle curve the shoreline of the bay.

Trevor Malcolm leant over the railing on the boat deck and gazed dejectedly at the pastel and terra cotta city across the widening expanse of turbulent water.

Carey would be on her way now, too, he mused—chatting happily to Gloria what's-her-face on the big blue tour bus; confiding, perhaps, that she'd met this terrible man. Aegean Sun Fun Tours triumphant, having reclaimed one of its long lost sheep. Not so long lost, really: three days, only. They'd known each other no longer than that. Or rather, *not* known each other. Blunders and cross-purposes—a hopeless *mésalliance*—from their walk to Selçuk after the accident in the Theatre till their parting at the Izmir Palas this morning. Three days during which they'd mostly been at odds with one another. Three days of misunderstandings on her part and frustration on his. He hated uncertainties, mysteries, falsely based opinions. And now he would have to live with the memory of all of these: not knowing the identity of the man he'd killed, not understanding the curious reaction of the Tourist Police in Selçuk, not having changed Carey's wrongheaded conviction that he was a bad lot.

He felt his sleeve tugged; and, turning, saw what he least expected. She was there, catching her breath as though she had just run all the way up the stairs of the Theatre at Ephesus!

Though he could not have been more astonished, or pleased, he managed to regard her up and down with an expression of mock severity. 'So you've done it again! Missed your bus! And I suppose you think I'll take you under my wing and put up with you and your oddities again, all the way to Istanbul—is that it? You complained that I was following you. Well, quite clearly it's you who's following me!'

She nodded weakly, unsmilingly.

'And you think I won't mind—'

Her eyes, abruptly charged with tears, pleaded with him to stop.

'Joking,' he said uncertainly. 'Only joking.—Carey, what the hell's wrong? What's happened?'

She stood unsteadily, swaying slightly, as if the ship were already at sea. She was so glad, so enormously relieved, to have found him. 'You were right!' she brought out, after a few moments.

'You were right and I was wrong, so wrong! Oh, Trevor, I'm sorry! And I'm frightened!'

He gripped her shoulders, stood frowning down into her face. 'Now, dry the eyes. And calm down. And stop doing that, stop apologizing. I'm not used to it. What the hell for?'

'I am apologizing! I need to. I want to.'

He shook her gently. 'Tell me what's happened.'

'To think that I might never have found you again, that you might have been left not knowing!'

'For godsake tell me!'

She glanced over her shoulder, then caught hold of his arm and turned him to the rail with her. 'Oh Trevor, Trevor—It's serious. And I'm frightened. I'll explain the whole thing later. But there's a man—or there was one—I recognized him. Don't do anything. Don't let him know we know. Just talk to me—'

She was startled by a gull's screaming and plummeting towards a handful of orange peel tossed by a passenger.

Curbing his impatience, he thought to calm her. 'There's the Izmir Palas, your old hotel,' he said, managing some lightness of tone, while wondering in slight alarm if there really had been, or still was, a man—and if this man was M. 'Pretty grand affair, that hotel. Three or four stars, I suppose. Mine usually don't have any.' What did she mean? What had she found out? He leant there, tensely, waiting, watching the city coil itself around the bay and flatten out and become more hazy beneath its mountain.

She was glad to feel him beside her, glad to feel his arm linked in hers. But her heart still pounded uncomfortably. 'There was a man,' she began at length, determinedly.

'Following you—?'

She slightly nodded. 'I don't know, but—'

'Men follow women here. Foreign women especially. The streets are full of men in Turkey, men with their worry beads and nothing to do but twiddle them. You know that. And Turkish ships are full of men.' He rattled on, to see if he could shake her belief in this man. 'Turkish women generally stay at home in this country, as the boar hunters said. You've noticed that, haven't you? Except in the cities. So there's a shortage.'

'I can't be sure he was following me. But he's on the ship.'

'You say you recognized him—?' This, he now saw, would seem to rule out M.

'The man from the restaurant in Selçuk. The man dining by

himself, remember? He sat down just after we did. Well, he's on this ship! I saw him just seconds before I found you.'

Trevor considered this 'The man from the restaurant—well, okay. And following you—'

She hesitated. 'I didn't say that, but—'

'He could easily be here, on this ship—innocently.'

'A coincidence—'

'Just that.'

'Yes,' she was forced to admit. 'I guess it could be coincidence. But—'

'Well, let's think about this a wee while. What's this fellow at the restaurant got to do with you? He had a right to be at the restaurant. Now he's going home. To his wife and kiddies in Istanbul. There's only a couple of restaurants in Selçuk, and there aren't many ships for Istanbul. It's not a great surprise for him to have taken this ship, just as we have. And I shouldn't think he'd any connection at all with M.'

'Maybe not—'

'Don't give the bugger another thought.' He felt glad of the man's being only the lone diner from Selçuk, eager to dismiss him from both their minds—as other, wholly pleasurable, implications of the present unexpected situation suggested themselves to him. 'If he's been following you it could only be from admiration of your matchless beauty, and I can't blame the poor fellow for that. He won't bother you when he knows you're with me.—Now, where's your cabin? In the first Class, of course—'

'I haven't got one—in the First Class or anywhere else.'

He laughed, she managed at last to smile.

'Well then—'

'Yes?'

'*I* just happen to have one, but—'

'Not in First Class.'

He slipped his arm around her waist and made her face him. Her heart leapt as his lips brushed hers, then returned. She felt herself brought all at once to a new level of vivid life, metamorphosed like a nymph in a myth. When she could draw breath she knew she wanted only to give herself to him.

Give herself to him—as that Lydian queen had given herself to Gyges, then compelled him to murder her husband, she suddenly thought. But what she was about to let happen would not entail anything approaching that. Mario wasn't here now, to be murdered; he would not know, would not be hurt.

The kiss had not come as a complete surprise; nor—strangely—had the eagerness of her own yielding. It flashed on her how she had been drawn all along towards apparent danger—while living unknowingly in a real one: her deciding to stay over in Selçuk, her treading the corridor of the Hotel Croesus like a sleepwalker past her own door to knock on his, her agreeing to dine at the *locanta* with him and see Aphrodisias, the city of love. All along she had not wanted to be on a bus with people from home. She remembered, and now recognized as a kind of hunger, that brief feeling of guilty joy she had experienced on saying good-bye to Mario at JFK.

She waited tensely with him at the rail, turned again towards the waves. The wind had risen. They were sailing westwards towards the open sea and a bank of purplish black clouds. At their backs sailors scrambled shouting from vehicle to vehicle, making sure of cables and chocs, shifting coils of rope, lashing canvases. The vessel had begun to pitch. The Muzak came more faintly now, vieing with the hiss and swoosh of waters. She was aware of his talking, in his low gruff tones, close to her ear; yet she took in little of what he was saying. Below decks the Third Class cabin beckoned with an urgency that intensified with each cresting wave. Her heart raced anew as she felt him straighten and drop his arm from around her waist. She followed him across the wet shining deck, climbing laboriously as the ship rose, tripping with forced lightness a few steps forward as it fell—telling herself mournfully, joyfully: It had to happen, though guilt and misery would come in its wake.—Guilt and misery, yet she could blame all this trouble, all her worry and fear, and even what was about to happen, on Mario—could she not? As she caught the door Trevor held for her she told herself Mario should have known better than to let her come to Turkey. He should have thought back that his own life had been threatened. It would've been his fault if she'd been killed at Ephesus.

The heavy door banged to behind her. She descended after him, clutching the cold rail—one set of stairs, then another. She trod a narrow and clammy corridor, rounded a corner after him, and, turning sharp, stepped over the iron threshold into the cabin. She felt a tingling excitement spreading from her lower back where his hand had been moments before, an intimate probing as though from tongues of fire licking her insides.

Rivets and running rust spots decorated the iron walls of the cabin, which contained an upper and lower bunk, a basin, a small table fixed to one wall, a chair. 'Nothing superfluous, as you see,' he commented. 'But there's a porthole, just on the waterline. And there's a sheet over the mattress, at least.' He talked with assumed casualness, while tense from the awareness that he was ready for her, the astonishing awareness that in a minute or so he would be next to her on the bed, with her. He noticed that his hand was shaking as he sought the zipper of his jacket.

Trying to concentrate on steadying her legs, against the motion of the ship, she stood facing him in the scanty space between the porthole and the bunks, taking in nothing of what he was saying, impatient to feel again his mouth on hers. He placed his hands on her shoulders, drew her to him, and began kissing her cheek and eyes—tasting the salt of her small tears as he had tasted the sea spray on deck moments before. 'It's very odd,' he murmured amusedly, 'but I want you. I didn't think I did, but I do. You're not at all what I've had in mind.'—Feeling his breath graze her ear she trembled violently. She thought that if it lasted another second, the waiting, if he did not come to her, she would sob hysterically and claw at the clothes he was only now taking off. She slipped off her top, helped him unsnag the zipper of her skirt, let the skirt fall. He moved against her, pushing her to the bunk and placing himself beside her. The legs, her legs were writhing, twining his, and now parting for him of their own accord; she had no desire to stop them.

'Now I'll tell you,' she said; and began by recounting her chance meeting with the boy in the lobby of the Izmir Palas.

There was no doubt in her mind that the 'friend' who had inquired about her there on Saturday afternoon was M, Trevor's M, the man he had encountered in Selçuk and before that at Ephesus on the path leading from the parking lot to the upper reaches of the Theatre. M might have spent the best part of an hour disposing of the body (helped by the youth in the beret, if he had anything to do with it? she wondered) and, as Trevor put it, 'cleaning up,' by which time Carey and Trevor would have been installed in their rooms at the Hotel Croesus. What he had made of the death of his accomplice could only be guessed at. Afterwards he would have pressed on alone, driven back to Izmir—that being the only place he knew her to be settled in. It was because M had spent the day in Izmir (thinking her again with the tour) that he had left her in peace on Saturday to wander around Ephesus as she pleased. Only when the bus returned without her from Cesmi and surrounding sites late that afternoon would he have learned from the boy that she had stayed on in Selçuk, and it was then that he had driven back and parked in the side street to keep watch on the Hotel Croesus. She supposed he would have killed her had Trevor not happened to see him, had the boar hunters not offered a means of escape, and had not she decided (for the wrong reasons) to go by van to Trobali, and thence by train to Izmir. 'So, you see, it was my life you saved that afternoon, with your little Swiss knife,' she concluded gravely.

'Well, I'm damned! But who—?'

She told him her husband had made enemies on his last business trip here, enemies who now thought to revenge themselves on him by killing her.

This explanation brought a raised eyebrow and a long whistle from her companion. 'Well, well. He must have done something truly … memorable, that husband of yours.'

'Terrible, is what you meant to say, isn't it?' She looked defiance. 'But no, it wasn't terrible. It really wasn't. I'll make you understand—'

'When was he last here, did you say?'

She sighed, and shook off the question. 'I went to the police in Izmir.'

'And?'

'I could see they didn't believe me, not entirely. And I suppose they are to be forgiven for thinking the threat, if it existed, less than I imagined.'

'How so?'

She did not answer immediately, as though some delay, some show of resistance, could put betrayal in a better light; as though willing to pretend to herself that betrayal had not already occurred, moments ago, here on a straw mattress in this third-class cabin on the *M.V. Izmir* .

He gave way to impatience, and leapt off at a tangent. 'And what about that message delivered to your tour bus guide, at the start of all this?'

She nodded, glad not to have to say, at least for now, what it was that Mario had done. 'The message I blamed you for. It must have been M who gave the boy in the parking lot at Ephesus the message for Kadir, telling him to go off without me.'

He silently agreed.

'To isolate me, I suppose. Give them all the time they wanted, or another opportunity in case the Theatre plan fell through.' She shuddered. 'Or else the fellow in the Theatre was going to shoot a drug into me, so M could kidnap me. Would that have been possible?—I don't know. Oh, Trevor, he knows when I'm due in Istanbul! And now he knows about the suitcase, the passport! He'll be waiting there for me. At the Istanbul Hilton.'

'He'll be waiting for *you,* yes—but not for *me.* We can be sure, now, that the reason he looked right through me at Selçluk was simply that he hasn't the faintest idea who I am and he doesn't care. Evidently he didn't get a good look at me on Mount Pion. He hasn't seen us together. He hasn't made the connection. He only knows and cares about you. So—'

'But Trevor—'

'*I'll* go for that suitcase, that passport.'

She raised her eyes to his. 'I don't want you hurt. If we could send for it, somehow—'

'I'll go. But Carey, you said the police in Izmir could be forgiven for thinking the threat less than you imagined. Why? And this "not terrible" thing your husband did, which was nevertheless enough to goad M and company to take revenge—'

'I'll have to phone him—phone Mario.'

'You're ducking the question.'

'It just occurred to me, that I should phone him.'

'Get him to intervene, you mean. Maybe make a deal with these "enemies." Call them off?'

'It had to do with an icon,' she blurted, in the face of this superciliousness. 'Do you know much about icons?'

He shook his head. 'Go on.'

'The police,' she began hesitantly. 'They might have gone after Mario, stirred things up, even after all this time. I didn't tell them everything. But I suppose I shall tell you.—I see it's necessary, much as I hate the idea of going against what I promised Mario; which was, never to tell anyone.'

He waited, gazing at her intently, while she thought how best to begin.

'Mario was, is, always ... correct,' she said quietly. 'Always fair. And above board. In business, I mean. But there was this one time, which wasn't his fault; which happened out of the blue, by chance.' Her eyes dropped from his. 'It had to do with an icon,' she repeated. 'A very valuable, fabulously valuable, icon of the Virgin—just head and shoulders, and no Christ child; a type called "Virgin without arms." It was classical, Byzantine, early twelfth century. Not just rare but unique, and in superb condition—on a slightly curved piece of some wood, olive I think. It had been taken from a family of Armenians, who died in the massacre you mentioned, and kept as a curiosity or trophy. It should never have left Turkey but got mixed up with some others by mistake, apparently. That's what Mario said. As a rule he didn't discuss his business with me, what he bought and what or to whom he sold, I mean. But he had to tell me about this because the money it brought presented a problem.'

'The amount.'

'Yes.'

'The root of all evil.'

'If that's what you choose to think—'

'He parked some of it with you.'

'He *gave* me quite a lot of it, yes. Invested it in my name. He's always been generous that way.'

'His Turkish contacts weren't delighted.'

'That was when he shelved the idea of returning to Turkey. He knew that if he ever did they would kill him.'

Trevor swung from the bunk's edge where he had been sitting, took several turns about the tiny cabin, and stood with his forehead pressed against the cold iron wall. 'And despite what happened, this husband of yours, Mario, was quite happy to let you come to Turkey—'

'It happened months ago, and I had nothing to do with it!—Mario never imagined I could be in danger!'

He returned to the bunk and settled himself beside her. 'If you say so,' he said, taking her hand. 'If you say so.'

The weather had worsened. The bow of the Izmir rose high, hung undecided, descended with a crash. When the stern rose in its turn the whole superstructure shook and clattered as the screws churned momentarily free of the depths.

'There've been announcements,' Carey said. 'Maybe we should've opened the door to listen. They might have been important.'

'Everything's in Turkish. We've just got to guess at what's happening. Not much, probably—times of dinner and breakfast, arrival time tomorrow; storm warnings, boat drill.'

'I don't care,' she said, her head cradled in his arm. 'I don't care about anything. I don't care now.—Do we get only one sheet? Just this one sheet that's covering this very thin straw mattress?—I've never had a straw mattress before.'

'There's a stack of wollen blankets up there,' he said, nodding to the bunk above.

'We could've had something better, less constricted, if that receptionist at the Palas had agreed to cash my cheque.—But as a matter of fact I'm quite content,' she quickly added.

'If she'd cashed your cheque that bell boy mightn't have got your ear and you'd have been on that bus, heading for the Izmir Hilton and M.—May I have my arm back? It's gone dead.' He swung his legs to the floor and staggered up. He went to the porthole, after colliding with the inside wall, and put his nose to the cold glass. No sky to be seen, just vallies and moving mountains of foaming green water. The seas of the Achaeans, of the Phoenicians, of Barbarossa the pirate. He returned, stepping over stray articles of clothing, to sit on the bunk edge again, and begin stroking and kissing her bare leg.

'Go on,' she murmured.

'And—?'

'Yes!'

'Higher still?'

'Yes, I—' She closed her eyes as his head dipped to kiss the insides of her knees, her thighs. He was wedging himself beside her as another public announcement sounded through the corridor outside. 'It's about dinner, probably.'

'Possibly the storm.'

'Mmm.'

'And it doesn't matter.'

'Oh no, it doesn't.'

The same message, whatever it was, crackled a second time over the public address system in the corridor.

'Please come again,' she said.

'Are you talking to me or it?'

'You,' she laughed softly.

Evening fell and the motion of the ship changed from pitching to rolling as she cleared the protective headland of Karaburun and swung her bows northwards towards the island of Lesbos.

Trevor and Carey dined happily aslant in their chairs amid the rattle of cutlery and the occasional tinkle of breaking wine glasses, congratulating themselves on being good sailors and noting with approval the abrupt departure of several diners; and, afterwards, when they made brief forays outside, rejoicing to find the decks deserted. They lived for present pleasure. For the time being the voyage was everything, the ship their world. Wind and wave abetted their zealous embrace of immediate event and sensation and seemed to diminish other danger. They heard the groaning and creaking of the ship and were content.

By morning the fury of wind and wave had spent itself; blue holes gaped in the cloud base and sunlight turned sections of gloomy sea to silverfoil. Passengers unseen before surfaced and strolled, too nonchalantly perhaps, on deck. Black-clad Turkish men smoked at the railings port and starboard; two teachers conducted a group of well-heeled schoolchildren to inspect the lifeboats and davits, the ventilators and cranes; a middle-aged English couple settled themselves at the base of the ship's funnel to read. Some time after breakfast Carey and Trevor found a purser who spoke English and who confirmed what had occurred to them over boiled eggs, *ekmek* and coffee: that the ship now ran several hours late because of the gale. She would not arrive in Istanbul before mid-day

With the blue line of coast in view, Trevor raised the subject of where they would stay. 'Not Beyoglu, the posh area, where all the banks and big hotels are. My former hotel, the Sahinlar, tucked away in the Old City, would be safe.'

'Third Class?' she teased.

'Of course. But it's new and clean and overlooks the Sea of Marmara. You can watch the seagulls and the ships while I'm fetching your suitcase.'

The smile that had appeared left her. Their brief idyll was ending. Sighing, she pulled his arm around her and settled herself against his chest. The thought that she ought to phone her husband recurred. Later, later. If only she'd taken the passport along with her to Ephesus instead of zipping it into the side pocket of the suitcase!—The contents of the suitcase didn't matter; they could be replaced in a day's shopping. But without her passport she was helpless. She could neither leave Turkey nor get money to live while she remained in the country. Being without money was a novelty and she hated it. Still, she dreaded Trevor's going for the passport, dreaded it in a way that brought to consciousness the surprising extent to which he had come to matter. And the pain in store for them both at their inevitable parting.

## Chapter 14

A SMOG-BROWN SKYLINE of mosques and minarets and coal-smoke-belching factories, rising from the choppy waters of the Sea of Marmara between an irregular line of anchored freighters: Istanbul—Earth's pearl, the city where Europe and Asia meet, the city of Byzas and Justinian, of Suleyman the Magnificent and Sultan Ahmet II. And now, mused Trevor, gazing with Carey from the bow deck of the M.V. *Izmir*, the city of M.

Aware of her nervousness he acted the voluble tour guide, a surrogate Kadir; pointing out for her the Sancta Sophia and the Blue Mosque, then the Topkapi Palace as the M.V. *Izmir* cleared Seraglio Point and slowed to approach the landing stage near the foot of the Galata Bridge.

As the ship nudged the wharf he made a move to join the press of passengers eager to disembark but felt her tug him back. 'Wait!' she implored. 'Let's watch and be sure there's no one.' And when the engines were shut down, the gangway lashed in place and the gates opened, she still hung back. He joined her now in scanning the dockside for the yellow Mercedes; then, fighting the contagion of her fear, he insisted on the near impossibility of M's being there to meet them. After all, how could anyone have even suspected their arrival by this means and at this hour?

Descending with the last passengers they made their way through the long low building housing the customs and shipping offices, only to find that traffic was at a choked and exhaust-drenched standstill, and that the few taxis on hand which had bothered to meet the ship at this late hour had all been taken.

'Rush hour,' he observed unnecessarily. '—Carey?'

She was squeezing his arm. 'Look, that man!'

He paled, thinking at once of M.

'He was in the restaurant, the ship—!'

Relieved, he exploded with: 'Oh, him! Only him!—Well, he's got to get off, the same as everyone else.'

She gave him an anxious glance.

'Come on,' he coaxed. 'You don't want to go on board again and get taken back to Izmir, do you? We can't stay here. And I think we can be sure that fellow, whoever he is, has nothing to do with you or me. So let's forget him. You say he stared at you in the restaurant; well, that's understandable. I don't blame him.'

'I wish we were being met by a limousine with bullet-proof glass.'

'Well instead of that we're walking. There are no taxis, and I hate them anyway. In that crowd it's not going to be easy for someone to follow us. The Sahinlar isn't far.'

His reasoning failed to reassure her and she followed him, pushing through the wall of others' welcomers, with an erratically beating heart. Almost everywhere she looked there were soldiers: on the quay, outside in the street and distantly in the porticos of important-looking buildings. The soldiers stood in twos and threes, alert and poised, legs apart, automatic weapons at the ready. To Carey the faces of the two who guarded the exit of the quay, and of two others at the foot of the bridge when they came to it, were eerily alike. Under their greenish helmets they wore an expression of robotic indifference; they gazed impassively from their slightly slanted eyes. From farther east, she thought; descendants of barbarian hordes, kin of the henchmen of Tamarlane.

'Don't worry about them,' said Trevor. 'Think of them as protection.'

'I hate them,' she returned with a shudder.

Traffic, vehicular jumbled with the pedestrian, streamed over the Galata Bridge. Trucks laden with produce ground forward, carts drawn by small lean horses lurched on a few paces at a time. Most of the cars were American or German models of twenty years ago. The crowds spilled over the pavements on both sides as they poured across the bridge. Men hung over the railings, fishing with rods made from coat hangers tied and bound to pieces of wood. The smell of fish rose from the tiny fish restaurants beneath the bridge and wafted from the embankment where mullet were being fried on coal fires. On either side of the bridge brightly painted *kayiks*, ark-like vessels with high prows and sterns, rode at anchor on the waters of the Golden Horn.

They worked their way across, intent on not losing one another among the throng of pedestrians, and entered the narrow twisting back streets belonging to the Old City on the other side.

The noise of traffic magically cut out. Their footsteps broke the silence of a cobbled lane that ran between high walls and balconies and ancient carved doors opening onto shaded courtyards. In one of these a child was playing handball by himself; in another three cats perched at improbably precise intervals in the leafless branches of a small tree, cleaning themselves. The lane yielded to a street of metal working shops, shops that were merely lean-tos under the arches of a wall, where men sat on rugs, tooling brass trays and hammering copper vessels.

Shattering the atmosphere of calm and sober industry, a car that had been parked ahead of them lurched suddenly down the curb and shot past with horn blaring and tires screaming. Shaken, Carey turned aside to pause in the doorway of a textile-maker's shop.

'They do that here,' said Trevor. 'It's a game: "Scare hell out of a foot-slogger today." The car is king.—You still in one piece?'

She was holding her breath and listening. 'Someone's coming. Someone's been following us.'

They heard approaching footsteps, and waited tensely. The footsteps ceased, began again, loudened.

A soldier strode by within a metre of them, looking neither to right nor left.

'I hate those soldiers,' she said, and was about to step forward when more footsteps sounded. From the doorway they watched, until a second figure passed.

'It was *him*!' hissed Carey. 'The man from the l*ocanta*—and the ship!'

'Are you sure? How could it be?'

'It was. I'm absolutely sure.'

This, now, he could not explain. He frowned. 'Well,' what the hell has he got to do with all this? With us? I don't understand.'

When all was silent he ventured forward. 'All clear. There's no one. We'll cut through that alley opposite and take a parallel street.' Without more words, they darted hand in hand for the alley. The street down which they turned at the end of it was almost as narrow, and not at all straightforwardly parallel.

'How in God's name do you know your way?' she inquired at length, strongly suspecting he didn't.

'The tower of the University. I can see it from time to time. I keep heading for that and hope to emerge eventually onto Ordu Caddesi, which is the main street.' He told himself he ought to feel more confident now. They'd cleared the ship safely and come this far. Could Carey have been mistaken about the fellow from the *locanta*? If not, he didn't know what to think. That the fellow should turn up again, here, was stretching coincidence too far; but if he really had been following them he'd overshot and lost them now.

The call of a *muezzin* welcomed them as they emerged onto Ordu Caddesi. Robed men were washing their feet at a small fountain before entering their mosque to pray.

'I'd better go tonight for the suitcase,' said Trevor as they waited to cross.

Carey reluctantly agreed. Gloria Bloomquist would be back with the tour about now, she thought.

Minutes later they passed thankfully through the doors of the Hotel Sahinlar and approached the desk. Dr Malcolm was recognised and made a fuss of. Most willingly were they given the room he had occupied when alone, a spacious room on the sixth and topmost floor, with double bed and bathroom. After the expected haggling, a price of two thousand liras was agreed on, the equivalent, Carey calculated with amazement, of only about twelve dollars. Everyone was friendly, from Abdu the chief desk clerk, to Ali Bey the boy of all works. Except for some slight show-offish eagerness on the part of Ali Bey, not the slightest awareness, let alone disapproval, was shown of Dr Malcolm's having acquired a companion on his latest expedition.

## Chapter 15

LEFT ALONE, AND feeling suddenly that it had been a mistake to let him go, she opened the door, hoping to find him still waiting for the lift. Instead she heard the whirr and creak of its descending. She had a sense of something—or someone—forgotten, left out of account. Not the lone diner from the *locanta* in Selçuk. A woman, rather. But no, this must come from her mistaken notion concerning the caller Trevor expected during the picnic dinner at the Hotel Croesus. At the end of the gloomy corridor a curtain twitched aside from the cupboard and she felt the eyes of the woman she had noticed there, squatting in the dark, ready to clean a room with her short straw broom. The corridor resounded with the deep voices, coughs and laughter of Turkish men, whose habit seemed to be to leave their doors ajar so they could continually drop in on each other and sustain the momentum of conversation and smoking.

He would be on the big avenue, Ordu Caddesi, by now, she thought, closing and re-locking the door.

She stepped out onto the small balcony and searched beyond the railing, shading her eyes against the setting sun. A few streets away the land ended. Beyond the cluttered rooftops of apartment buildings several ships lay at anchor, enveloped in a brown and purple haze. The balcony did not face the way Trevor had gone. He'd said the bridge, the new part of town they called Beyoglu, and the streets leading to the Hilton, all lay on the other side.

She thought once more of phoning her husband. She must do so when Trevor safely returned. She owed it to herself, supposing him able to shed light on M; but was she at the same time secretly hoping for a minor miracle, that his learning of M and identifying him would ironically result not only in M's arrest, but in her being able to spend a few more days with Trevor, free from danger? If so, she was surely dreaming. Besides, what was the good of their having a few more days together?

Into her face and lungs coal smoke gusted from the next rooftop. Holding her breath she re-entered the room.

The maid would wonder at her having no clothes piled on the shelves or hung in the bathroom. Trevor's backpack, open and with a pullover hanging from it, occupied the armchair. She placed it on the floor beside the battered brown suitcase which he had last night retrieved from the care of Ali Bey and settled herself in the chair. Her gaze fell on the Marks & Spencer bag, its colour almost bleached out. She rose, fished from it the Swiss knife, and returned to the armchair.

Comparisons, thought Carey, staring at the knife, can never be more odious than where a husband and a lover are concerned. The two placed themselves next to one another in her mind, however. The smooth alongside the rough, the tried and true alongside a still largely unknown quantity. The one had long provided her with a comfortable life; the other had obliviously saved it. She was hard-pressed to fault her kindly, even-tempered, and generous, husband; the other had shown her all too nakedly his curmudgeonly side. She knew he could be gruff and grumpy, even when he had not just murdered someone. She had never been afraid of Mario. Yet only yesterday—was it, or the day before?—she had deemed Trevor dangerous; she had feared, hated, him.

Fancifully, fleetingly, she had even equated him with Gyges; felt obscurely that he posed some similar danger to her husband, several thousand miles away on a different continent. Lingering over the thought, while still clutching the knife, she looked down to see that her fingernail had found the convenient groove and opened the main blade.

It was an incomprehensible thing, her love—like infinity or a peacefully simmering saucepan of milk that had violently boiled over when her back had been turned. She fondly recalled the paper bag picnic, which had not been altogether pleasant at the time; also the excitement he stirred in her when he described Aphrodisias. She imagined him teaching her what to look for there, how to deal with the shards, the bits of figurines, that came to light at Aphrodisias. Her life as it might have been, she told herself with some sadness.

Suddenly she wanted desperately to blame her husband, as though that might do some good. She imagined herself phoning and remonstrating with him, working herself up to being angry with him, angry for arranging this trip to Turkey—when he knew he had enemies here. 'You didn't *think*,' she heard herself saying.

'You were too busy to think of me, and of what might happen to me. You should have remembered; you should have known these people you cheated might take it out on me.' At once she was aghast at the words which streamed through her mind, and knew she could never utter them. It was all far-fetched, monstrously unfair. He could never have dreamed of these people even finding out she was here. And hadn't he always been good to her? He was blameless, and she knew she could never leave him. The wife seeking desperately to justify her disloyalty, her betrayal—that was what it amounted to.

Yet she did not love her husband. She knew that now. Her mind reached out to Trevor in a fever of impatience, and irritation. He had given her no promise that he would on this occasion take a taxi. Why was he so silly about taxis?

* * * * *

'I'm here to see a Mrs Bloom—' Trevor began, but the telephone rang at the far end of the counter and the receptionist, a short doe-eyed young woman with soft rounded features, apologized with a look that said he should admire her, and skipped to answer it.

He had strode from the hotel entrance directly to the front desk, looking neither to right nor left; now he swung round and surveyed, with a mixture of nervousness and defiance, the present occupants of the lobby. All seemed to be tourists or members of the hotel staff. He glanced at his watch. Concern for Carey's impatience had prompted him to hail a taxi on Ordu Caddesi after all. He would get back early and surprise her.

'Sorry about that, Sir! You were saying—?' The doe eyes and full-lipped mouth were smiling, the head of pony-tailed black hair tipped like that of a child eager to please.

'Yes, I've come to see a Mrs Bloomquist. Would you tell me her room number?'

'Mrs Bloomquist—with Aegean Sun Fun Tours. She is away until the day after tomorrow, Sir.'

'Away? But—'

'A two-day tour to the Black Sea. Their itinerary was changed; I believe because the ship they were scheduled to take in a day or so collided with a freighter and needed repairs.—Ah! I haven't explained that clearly, have I?'

'Not clearly, no,' Trevor responded. 'But never mind.'—Damn! he thought. What now?—'I'm here on behalf of a Mrs Signorello,' he briskly pressed on. 'She left her suitcase in the care of Mrs

Bloomquist a couple of days ago and now she needs it—badly. She's asked me to collect it.'

The girl explained that Mrs Bloomquist had brought the suitcase down for safekeeping when she left, because the room was to be given up and a different one assigned for her return. Through a door behind the desk he could see a double row of suitcases awaiting collection.

'And you are Mr Signorello,' declared the receptionist brightly—and too loudly for his liking.

All would have been well had he been canny enough to stop himself from denying the fact. He gave his name. 'I'm a friend. I see the suitcases are through there. Shouldn't be too difficult to find Mrs Signorello's.'

She turned and went through to the suitcases, taking quick little steps in her high heels and short tight skirt. He watched her through the partially open door as she stooped to read the labels of the suitcases, swinging her locked knees from side to side as she manoeuvered. She rose, brushed her skirt back down as far as its brevity would allow, and popped out, smiling afresh, to ask what colour Mrs Signorello's suitcase was.—Colour? He had no idea. Carey hadn't told him. With a mildly disapproving glance, the girl ducked back—reappearing moments later to set down of her side of the counter a blue Samsonite suitcase. A frown announced that with the suitcase found she must take the whole matter more seriously. She must, she now told him, seek the authority of someone more senior than herself, before letting it go. The office was just upstairs; she would ring and someone would come down at once. He watched her slip to the end of the counter and pick up the phone. Patience. It would be all right. The manager or whoever it was could phone Carey. Ah, but would he accept her being who she said she was, not insist on her coming in person, not require some piece of written identification from him at least?

He swiveled and surveyed the lobby once more. A large woman in a pink track suit was fussing over a Yorkshire Terrier. As she moved away, his eye fell on a man staring at the ceiling from a sofa. Something about the studied nonchalance made him uneasy. Had he been there a minute before, obscured by a column—slumped, too indolently perhaps, his knees high and wide apart, twirling in one hand a string of worry-beads? Following the man's gaze to the ceiling Trevor could discover in its lofty creaminess nothing whatever of interest.

'The line is busy, sir.' The receptionist had tapped his arm. 'If you wouldn't mind waiting I'll run up and fetch someone.'

But suppose this someone decides not to authorize the thing, my little Turkish delight? Then what?—His eyes left the pony-tail of black hair swinging to and fro across her back as she walked towards a sign saying 'Service Elevator.' The sofa was now empty, the man with the worry beads and the ceiling fixation was nowhere to be seen. Could he have been M? Trevor sharply regretted not having raised his eyes to him from the path on Mount Pion, and only glimpsing him in the darkness of the street in Selçuk.

Simultaneously he awoke to the fact that he was alone and within reach of the suitcase. Yes, of course the manager would want some authority, a letter from Carey. They'd been daft not to think of that. A doorman was talking to a newly-arrived couple at the far end of the lobby. Near at hand there was no one: no one at the cash, no one behind the counter. A swing gate was all that separated him from the suitcase. He could see the zipped-up outer pocket where the passport was. *Take that*, he thought. *Just that*! The suitcase could stay.

His knee nudged the swing gate; he slipped into the inner office; his fingers found the zipper, then the passport. Moments later he was through the main door of the hotel and taking the steps two at a time.

But Christ! Where were the taxis? Not one at the Hilton! And just when he'd condescend again to take one!—He slowed, caught his breath, told himself he should walk normally, not attract attention. What was the rush, after all? In the hotel they'd wonder why he'd decided not to hang around—maybe put it down to Anglo impatience. But the passport wouldn't be missed.

Emerging from the hotel driveway onto Muriyet Caddesi he turned to see standing on the hotel steps a figure resembling that of the man on the sofa. The next moment he collided with something—with some*one*, rather: a woman, a woman who had popped into his path from behind a kiosk. The impact sent her down, a lanky figure sprawling at his feet with the finality of a slain giraffe.

He thought afterwards it must have been the oaths breaking from him that prompted her to scold in English.

'So clumsy you are! Rush, rush! This is sidewalk, no?—not *Autobahn*!'

He was helping her up, mouthing apologies, restraining with difficulty his frustration and fury. 'Can you walk?'—Throwing another backwards glance, he was relieved to see the man on the steps turn and re-enter the hotel.

'I don't know.—Oh!'

He stood in a frenzy of impatience, silently cursing the woman for stepping in his way, and strongly tempted to abandon her and dash for the line of taxis. Anxiously, he watched her teetering experimentally before him: a large-boned woman in her late thirties, an ugly-sexy woman, whose face had a mask-like quality of exaggerated feature; her voice deep, a smoker's voice; her accent thick. 'Try to walk,' he insisted.

Steadying herself, she plunged a hand into her open shoulder bag and found a stubby pencil and an envelope. 'In case there is damage to me, your hotel and room number, please?'

He gave them, then handed her a pair of dark glasses that had been knocked off in the fall. Taking them with one hand she dabbed with the back of the other her black eyes, gently so as not to disturb the long false lashes and the mascara. A frown showed through the fringe of dusky hair, a lop-sided smile tugged at the corners of the large rubbery lips. 'I need you arm,' she said. 'My car is that one.'

'I'm in a bit of a hurry—', he protested.

'Your arm,' she insisted. 'My car is just there.' She swung her bag to indicate a long emerald green Chrysler, a vehicle dating from the days of overblown bodywork, fins and stuck-on chrome. 'I am okay. You could not help it, I think.' She sighed, shot him a glance that hinted at forgiveness. 'The kiosk, it was—how you say?—a blind point.'

'Blind spot, yes. Yes, it was. Now I must—'

'Do you want taxi? Of course you want. So you get in. I be your taxi.' She scrabbled in her shoulder bag for the car keys and swung open the door for him. 'You cross the bridge to the Old City? Your hotel is there—'

Well, why not? Better than a taxi. All he needed was to get clear of this area, get back eventually to Carey. A lucky accident, then.—As they drew away he looked back a last time. The hotel entrance stood empty. Apparently none of the staff had taken the slightest interest in his departure. And perhaps the man on the sofa, or on the steps, wasn't M. He fetched a deep breath and let it out slowly; he felt his heartbeats returning to something like their normal rate. He smiled inwardly, reflecting on the woman's securing his address while forgetting to ask his name. 'Nice car,' he said.

'You like my car?—But it is too big, for parking. And the petrol!—I prefer my motorcycle.'

'Motorcycle? Here, in Istanbul?—You have courage.'

She laughed. 'And do you leave Istanbul, in such a hurry and in such a beautiful weather?' The voice of his companion roused something unexpected in him—her purring, slow voice, a voice that had a strangely arresting *timbre*. 'You may use my name,' she added, smiling her pliable smile aside while changing lanes. 'Roxelana—okay?'

'I'll be here a while yet,' he answered shortly.

They coasted down the wide tree-lined avenue. Traffic had thickened. Like most of her nation, Roxelana drove with zest—accelerating towards the back of any car in her way, braking as late as possible, and not slowing, not braking at all, of course, for pedestrians. Crossing Taksim Square she declared: 'I need *khave*—coffee; you will not mind'—and without waiting for his reply swung the wheel and sped along a side street, accelerating in response to the additional challenge of unpredictable pedestrian traffic and the street's narrow and twisting character. Thankful at least that she had driven fast and turned abruptly from the main road, confident that no one had followed, he swallowed his protest. As she geared down, hurtled round another corner and bumped the Chrysler half up on the narrow pavement a little beyond a sign that read *Bar-Kafeterya*, he thought resignedly: Having taken that taxi to get to the Hilton I'm running early so far as getting back to Carey is concerned. She can't be expecting me for a while. A few more minutes here won't matter. And I've got the passport.

'It is a small place I know,' said Roxelana conspiratorially, getting out and leading him through a low open doorway into a pungently smoke-laden room. 'You sit, okay?—I come back.'

He found a table near a window and occupied himself blowing from the tablecloth several dead leaves shed by an anaemic-looking lemon tree that sprouted listlessly from a cracked amphora. He watched the woman, Roxelana, speaking to the tatooed café owner, then walking towards a corridor. She had lost her limp. Apart from a group of old men playing a game in a far corner, and a red-eyed underslept-looking Dalmation, the café was empty. From the window the Chrysler lay out of sight in the gathering darkness a short distance down the street.

His strange companion reappeared. She wore a black leather jacket and grey slacks. He noted as she sat down that she had touched up her lips and sprayed her blouse with perfume reminiscent of hyacinths past their prime. 'I have ordered *khave* and raki,' she announced in her throaty voice, her long fingers flitting briefly to his arm. 'Okay?'

'Quite okay, if it won't take too long.' What's so sexy about an ugly, rubber-mouthed monstrosity? he wondered. He couldn't see the legs. And the clothes enhanced none of the usual features. The voice, then—the voice that was undeniably enticing; together with the deep-set, soul-struck eyes, eyes that were large even before art made them theatrically enormous with encircling shadows of purple and black.

'Too long?' she laughed wheezily. 'Too long!—What is too long? You have *khave* with a Turkish woman and you say is too long!' She glanced at him reproachfully, lit a cigarette, inhaled deeply, then aimed the contents of her doubtlessly blackened lungs aside at the sun-bleached wallpaper.

'Sorry.'

'Ah, ah, ah—no more apologize. Friends now, no?—We say we bumped into one another, you and I! We met by *accident*!' The rubber mouth mimed a guffaw. The teeth were terrible. He cringed inwardly at the appalling level of her humour, yet something in him stirred. She talked on unhurriedly, posing predictable questions, paying little attention to his brief replies. The café owner brought coffee and two small glasses of raki.

So here I am, thought Trevor, lumped with this superannuated siren, this caricature *houri*, and now, of all times! Yes, here's my 'Oriental Experience,' the Turkish *affaire* that's been missing in my life, the 'Oriental Experience' I promised myself! Here it is, in this grotesque form, and when it's most *mal à propos*!—Well, it serves me right for wanting it, instead of something like Carey!

The café man was signaling.

'What a nuisance,' said Roxelana, rising at once. 'It is a telephone call for me.'

Someone, thought Trevor smiling, must know her haunts.

Rejoining him minutes later, she peremptorily signaled an encore of coffee and raki, lit another cigarette, inhaled, and proceeded to tell him about her namesake, Roxelana, the daughter of a Russian priest—'taken very young into the harem of Topkapi to please the sultan, Suleyman the Magnificent.'

During the pause that accompanied the arrival of the second

round of coffee and raki Trevor glanced uneasily at his watch. 'I must go,' he said. 'I'm expected.'

'She was very beautiful, and intelligent,' his companion persevered obliviously. 'And ambitious, of course. By poisoning her rivals she became his sultana.' Her chin dropped briefly to her breastbone, the long lashes played hide-and-seek behind a curtain of glossy hair. 'It was she who persuaded Suleyman to arrange the disappearance of each of his sons. One son, then another, then another. All, in fact, except the son she had by him!' The rubbery lips drew apart to expose the ranks of tobacco-stained teeth.

'Ah.'—Was it the ominous twist to the story or the woman's having imperiously ordered that second round of coffee and raki that now made him uneasy? As he asked himself this question he watched her take from her bag, clean the dust from, and then put on (apparently in defence against no more than a distant lightbulb), the pair of dark glasses that had fallen when she had crashed to the pavement by the kiosk on Muriyet Caddesi. A shock ran through him. The dark glasses brought back the gangly 'youth' in the parking lot at Ephesus.

He tumbled to everything at once. M had left the sofa to phone Roxelana at the kiosk, alert her to his approach, and get her to stage the accident on Muriyet Caddesi, knowing she could use this as an excuse to learn his and Carey's address—the address he would now have, after phoning her again!

He struggled to conceal the added agitation the revelation produced in him.—I must leave at once, he told himself. I must get to Carey before M does!

'Something is wrong?'

The shock showed. 'No, no—,' he faltered, seeking desperately some tactic that would save him, save Carey.

'But—'

He caught the suspicion, the menace, in her glance. He could neither think nor act. Roxelana might have been a cobra and he its mesmerised prey. Oddly, it was her perfume that saved him, bringing with it the notion of sex.

'Something is wrong,' she repeated.

'Yes, I—'

She showed no sign of emotion in her eyes, or still smiling mouth, but revealed it to him in a certain muscular tension.

'That scent, the perfume you're wearing—what is it?'

The question achieved total surprise, surprise which held her silent some seconds. 'I forget the name, You don't like it?'

He fetched a deep significant breath, shifted forward and slid both his hands half across the table as though readying them to assault her breasts. The extreme danger had brought clarity, the certainty that audacity alone could save him. Energy and strength of purpose concentrated themselves in his eyes as he leant towards her now. The arteries in his neck bulged and pounded.

'I like the sent, the perfume. I wish you could remember its name. But it was that that made things go wrong. I mean, it's made me ... go off the rails a little.' He managed a laugh.

'Off the rails?' She was watching him narrowly, now.

'Turned my head a bit, unsettled me. It's so ... Eastern, Oriental. It suggests things exotic, sensual, forbidden perhaps.' He quickly explained that he was in Turkey as an archaeologist but that he'd had all along a secret desire to have a love affair with a Turkish woman; to have what he cherished in his imagination, dreamed, as an *affaire à la Turque*. He fastened his eyes to hers; he would not let them go. 'You see I was disillusioned. Women in the West have become... difficult,' he continued. He'd had his fill of assertive, independent, domineering, women. Suzanne, the woman he'd married, was typical: materialistic, calculating, ambitious. (No sooner had he used the word 'ambitious' than he bit his tongue, recalling Roxelana's implicit approval of her namesake's success story.) 'Ironically,' he hurried on, 'instead of that I've gotten myself involved with just the sort of assertive, independent, materialistic, domineering woman I wanted to avoid—a typical Western type, a typical American female! She attached herself to me like a limpet a few days back and since then I've had nothing but trouble. Nothing but trouble! Now she's treating me like an errand boy!'—Poor Carey!

Seeing the corners of his companion's lips starting up in a slow, much broader, smile, he pressed on forcefully. 'What you must understand, Roxelana, is that I've never known an Eastern woman.'

She asked his name, then dropped her eyes to where one of her hands lay extended, invitingly close to his on the table.

'I hope I'm not offending you, Roxelana. I hope I'm not shocking you. But there is something in you—and that scent—which has made me confess this to you.'

'You wanted a Turkish woman—' she rejoined at length, amused and at the same time impressed.

'Yes, but I found that they were sheltered. It was almost impossible for me ... for any degree, even slight, of ... penetration.' He seized her hand. The action brought with it the confirmation of arousal; and, oddly, the realization that he was exciting himself as well. Within seconds he felt her forefinger suggestively caressing his cupped palm. 'Our accident today, our collision—'

She withdrew her hand and, with a laugh, raised it to cover her mouth—newly conscious, perhaps, of the chaotic ranks of teeth and wishing to hide them. 'Silly boy!' she said. 'What a silly boy you are.'

'Roxelana,' he persisted, boring into her with his eyes, 'our meeting was *meant*.' (By M, it was, he put in grimly to himself.) 'You know I want you.'

'But how excitable my boy is!'

'You excite me.'

Her smile was now a leer.

Trevor hesitated significantly before bringing out: 'Surely, Roxelana, in Istanbul, we could lose ourselves, manage a discrete affair?'

'Turkish men are very jealous. I am married. Are you not afraid?'

'Roxelana!—No one needs to know! No one! Ever!'

'My husband ... he is not often with me these days, it is true—'

'Ah!'

'So ... persuading!'

The onslaught had shaken her up. He could see that. It had served its purpose. He was safe, for the moment at least. His mind leapt forward, sought some means of escape.

'I am married,' she repeated. 'I must ... consider.'

'But of course!'—Escape won't be enough, he told himself. By now M would be on his way to the Sahinlar. How was he to get there before M?

'It is sudden—'

'I admit that.'

'We would have to find ... a safe place. Some safe place to go.'

'Yes!' He could see her thinking.

'Arrange a time.' She laid her hand on his arm. Her eyes ran over him approvingly.

Christ! he thought. She's serious. Dead serious. But now—

'Arrange a time—'

Plunging his hand into the bag hanging on the chairback where the car keys were wouldn't get him far. She'd be after him and so would her friend the café man. Something else. Another way out, besides that door. For which he'd need a distraction, something that would buy time.—His eye fell on the various cakes displayed in a glass case at the inner end of the dining room. 'We must talk,' he said. 'Now that I've got something to stay for. Over another raki? And cake—one of those pastries? Let me buy you a pastry. He half rose, then seated himself determinedly. 'I don't know anything about Turkish pastries. Not a thing. And I don't speak the language.' He dug out his wallet and thrust a five hundred lira note into her hand—hoping this would deter her from taking her shoulder bag to the counter. 'Please, do the honours. Choose for us a *spécialité de la maison*—one for each of us.' He met her eyes unwaveringly as she hesitated.

'Very well,' she said.

The bag still hung on the chair back. His one chance. And Carey's.

She rose. He waited only until her back was turned to reach out the car keys from the bag across form him. Pocketing them he sprang to join her at the counter.

'Back in a minute,' he said and strolled past her to the corridor where the washrooms were. Once out of sight and free to explore he poked his head into the men's *tuvalet*—only to curse the lack of a window; He tried the room beside it, a storage room cluttered with empty barrels and boxes. Here there was a window, partly open. He entered the room and closed the door behind him. The window offered no resistance. He heard a noise at his back and turned to see the café owner advancing on him with a broken wine bottle in his hand. Toppling a barrel in the man's path gave him just enough time to get through the window and drop down free into the street.

He sprinted for the Chrysler and tumbled in, started up and reversed with squealing tires up the side street to where he could turn. He glimpsed Roxelana in the lighted doorway of the café. Heart thumping wildly, he regained the avenue, got his bearings and joined one of the lines of vehicles heading down to the Galata Bridge. He guided the big car over the bridge and soon broke out of the back streets of the old city to emerge on Ordu Caddesi. Moments later, having cut over in time for the turn at Lalele, he brought the vehicle hard over the curb opposite the Hotel Sahinlar, tore the handbrake up and leapt out. At the lift he stood clenching his fists and silently praying to Artemis as it descended, groaning and creaking, to collect him.

# Chapter 16

'BUT WHERE CAN we go?' cried Carey. His breathless explanation had coincided with the loudening clamour of the lift re-ascending. They were only half-way down the dim corridor when the lift door clanged open. There appeared, however, not M but the masked cleaning woman, bent on scurrying to her broom cupboard. They dodged past her to the emergency door. The concrete interior of the stairwell amplified their footsteps and threw off echoes, a din sufficient to make them imagine an army of pursuers.

'I've got hold of a car.' Trevor plunged out into the darkness and halted, momentarily disoriented. 'Don't ask me how.—*There*!'

The antiquated Chrysler stood nosed into a pile of rubble where he had left it.

'Trevor!' Her grip tightened on his arm.

A man stood beside the car, his bald head catching the lamplight, his arms akimbo. Even as they shrank back, he turned.

They fled down a narrow street through pools of moonlight and ragged shadow, stumbling over potholes and skirting piles of rubble and parked cars. Ahead rose a wall; the street was a dead end.

'Back there!' cried Carey. 'We passed something!' A foot passage, snaking off between overhanging hovels, a passage close and mean, suggestive of a drainage ditch between banks of mud—leading where? The sound of approaching footsteps sent them headlong down it, startling into howls and driving before them a pack of foraging dogs. Ahead danced a patch of light. Nearing it they heard music and the noise of a crowd, and seconds later they burst from the passageway into an open square filled with people, people engrossed in the spectacle before them, the spectacle of a traditional folk dance. To the music of wooden flutes and primitive drums, men in black pantaloons and trailing scarlet sashes leaped and whirled, circling a core of young women in long white gowns holding candles. Onlookers in the street clapped and cheered the dancers on with cries of *Yasha*! *Yasha*!—bravo! Old people and children leant from balconies, shouting encouragement.

Searching for the soldiers he knew must be there, as at every crowd scene in Turkey these days, Trevor saw the barrel of an assault rifle protruding from the shadows not twenty metres further on: a soldier, stationing himself half hidden, part-way up a flight of steps.

Glancing over her shoulder, Carey glimpsed their pursuer emerging from the passageway they had just left. Her scream brought the soldier down the steps in a bound, and into the open—into the open and into full view of the man, who turned at once, intent on retreat.

'Terrorist!' bellowed Trevor at the soldier, and flung his arm back at the man. 'Assassin!'

They saw the man pitch forward, go down as though flung. Was it Carey's imagination, or did the music of the flutes and drums falter, briefly dissonant in deference to the event? She was next aware of Trevor's encircling arms.

'Didn't I tell you these soldiers weren't so bad?'

She forced a smile.

He turned her face up to his and kissed her.

'I don't know,' she said. 'Maybe he'd just as soon have shot us if you hadn't pointed.'

They saw the soldier joined by two others.

'Everyone is behaving as though nothing has happened,' observed Carey.

'Afraid to get involved.'

'And those three are just standing there, over the body. Isn't it odd, how they're ignoring us?'

'Not for long, I think.'

A minute later they were wordlessly motioned to a car which had drawn up at the side of the square. It was a disquietingly unofficial-looking, dented, out of date car, from which a stocky, pock-marked, man sprang, to flash what might have been an identity card, and open the rear door for them to get in. As they sped off Trevor rapped on the heavy glass shield separating them from their escorts and shouted: 'Who are you?' An over-the-shoulder answer, muffled, in Turkish, unintelligible, was returned. 'Don't worry,' he said, settling back and taking her hand. 'They must be official. Otherwise our soldier boy would have shot them too.'

'There are no door handles!' was Carey's reply.

The car hurtled through poorly lit streets, cornering with shrieking tires, on a journey that was mercifully short but frightening. Carey was on the point of explaining about Mario: how she'd phoned, but she was prevented by a sentence in Turkish bawled from the front seat and signaling their arrival. Transferred to the gloomy interior of a building guarded by several soldiers, they were hurried to a narrow, smoke-filled office. A man with hooded eyes and a dueling scar on his right cheek nodded them languidly to two upright chairs set before his desk and gazed at each in turn from behind an ashtray piled high with cigarette butts. He waited until joined by a young woman, who sat down and prepared herself to take notes; then introduced himself as Colonel Akif of Military Intelligence. After which, to Carey's slight surprise, he turned his attention, not to her but to Trevor.

'Mr Malcolm—or *Dr* Malcolm, I should say.'

'You could, but it doesn't matter.'

'Doesn't it?' Through a set smile he spoke an English that was clipped, precise, correct. 'Ah, you in Scotland are natural democrats. No nonsense about titles. Still, I respect a title when it has been earned—from the University of Edinburgh, I understand. As you see, I have made it my business to find out something about you. Now, however, I wish you to tell me more. A good deal more.'

'I'm an archaeologist.'

'That I knew already. You are an archaeologist, and—?'

'And what?—You mean the site, my work? I'm digging at Aphrodisias.'

The Colonel's smile sagged. 'Dr Malcolm, let us not waste time. I have certain obvious questions. Who are you really? And why are you here?'

Carey could not help wondering if she was about to discover more about her friend, something he had omitted to tell her.

'Dr Malcolm,' pursued the Colonel. 'It is in your interest to oblige me with the truth. If you do not—'

'I'm an archaeologist, with government permission to dig at Aphrodisias. My papers are all in order. They're in my case, back at the hotel. I'm with Dr Edrim of the University here. Ask him, if you like.'

His interlocutor sighed heavily. 'Try harder, please. Your situation is not at present an enviable one, Dr Malcolm. Let us begin, not with Aphrodisias but with Ephesus.'

'Ephesus—' He felt a tremor of guilt, of fear. So the bastard knew about that.

'Yes, Ephesus. There, in the Theatre, three days ago, you killed a man. A man named Gokalp.'

Trevor said nothing.

'We wanted him, but you got there first.'

'Got there first?' Trevor blurted in consternation. 'I don't know what you mean. All I know is that he attacked me!'

Akif smiled imperturbably. 'Our people had been following him. You knew that. Alas, we came too late—only in time to fetch, identify and dispose of the body. And also, of course, to leave the place tidy, for the tourists.'

'I went to the Tourist Police in Selçuk. I told them everything!'

'Yes, I know.'

'It didn't occur to you to tell your friends there what you've just told me?'

'They are not my friends—'

'Colleagues, then.'

'From them I learned of you, Dr Malcolm. It was perhaps ungrateful of me not to supply them with information in return. I had, however, good reasons not to.—But as I was saying, at Ephesus you killed Gokalp. And here, Dr Malcolm, here not an hour ago, you were, it seems, responsible for the death of a second man—a man named Merlana.'

'Responsible!—I shouted at the soldier, that's all!'

'It sufficed, that shout,' remarked the Colonel. 'Deftly, tellingly, delivered. The timing quite perfect. You led him to the square, where you knew there would be soldiers, helpful soldiers.'

Carey asked herself if it was the gun she thought she had seen in the man's hand that had prompted the soldier to fire. Had he understood Trevor's shout, or had her own scream been enough? In any case she couldn't bear another minute the way everything was being misunderstood. 'Captain Akif, please!' she cut in.

'Colonel,' he corrected, raising a hand to silence her and pressing on: 'I don't take kindly to the loss of this Merlana, Dr Malcolm. He would have been as valuable to me as Gokalp.'

'He was out to kill Mrs Signorello! Me too, probably,' protested Trevor. 'He had a gun.'

Colonel Akif assumed a set smile and continued. 'Let us leave that for the moment.—You knew as well as I that both men were simultaneously attached to the Tourist Police of Anatolia and to the Turkish Mafia—'

Trevor vigorously shook his head.

The hooded eyes narrowed; the smile vanished. 'You deny it?—Now, tread carefully, Dr Malcolm. I know more than you think, and it would not do to lie to me.'

Unable to contain himself, Trevor rose, took a few steps from the desk, then returned. 'Colonel Akif, I haven't the slightest idea what you're talking about. I can't help it if you don't believe what I'm saying. The fellow at Ephesus attacked me, tried to kill me. I had no idea who he was. I surprised him in the act of putting together a rifle. We struggled. I had to defend myself. The other one, this Merlana, his pal, caught up with us here.'

Akif stubbed out his cigarette and leisurely lit another. 'Consider, Dr Malcolm: two key members of a criminal organization are eliminated, Gokalp then Merlana, in different places, one after the other, and the only common link between the two events appears to be yourself. Gokalp was eliminated by you directly, Merlana through you indirectly. Is it any wonder I should want to know more about you?'

'Colonel, I have something to say!' cried Carey. 'You must listen!'

'Mrs Signorello, I will come to you presently—'

'No! You will come to me now!' insisted Carey, anger and indignation lending her courage. 'You ignore women in your country but you're not going to ignore me. *I'm* the one you should've started with. I'm the one you should be putting these questions to! All this is stupid. You've been wasting your time. It's all about me, this whole thing! *Me*! Just listen—you've got to listen!'

This time the other merely closed his eyes, as if to shut her from his presence. 'Calm yourself,' he said after a moment. 'You are hysterical.'

'I'm not hysterical!'

The Colonel lit a cigarette, sighed, and rocked back in his chair. 'Very well. But please be brief.'

'I'm the wife of Mario Signorello,' she began determinedly; and went on to explain about her husband, about his arranging for her to tour Turkey and Greece, and about her coming close to being killed at Ephesus and again here in Istanbul. She had found herself to have been the intended target. Mr Malcolm—Dr Malcolm—far from being directly involved, was an innocent bystander who happened to have saved her life. She could not be sure as to the motive of the man or men who had hired Gokalp and Merlana to kill her, but she had come to suspect that it had to do with a business transaction of her husband's, a transaction which had apparently not been to the advantage of people here.

Akif was now looking at her steadily. 'Mario Signorello—.' He sat forward. 'Go on,' he said quietly. 'I am listening. Explain.'

'Well, some time last year, I forget just when, he came here, came to Turkey, and negotiated a shipment of antique weapons, jewellery and the like. He'd come before, a couple of times. That's his business, dealing in antiques—especially from the Middle East. As a rule he doesn't talk much with me about his business, but he told me about an icon. It's value was found to be a lot more than the sellers had thought, but he said it was a done deal and refused to make any adjustment to the purchase price.'

'And you think—'

'Well, yes. Of course. I remembered that. And it's the only explanation, isn't it? Someone here who had it in for Mario found out about my coming.'

At the name of Carey's husband and on a sign from the Colonel the woman taking notes had risen and left the room; she now returned, said something close to the ear of her superior, and resumed her place. In the silence following Carey's account Colonel Akif sat, leaning back now, smoking and occasionally running an index finger up and own the scar on his cheek.

'My husband is coming here,' added Carey a minute later, with a troubled glance aside at Trevor. 'I phoned. I felt I had to, after all that's happened. He's … worried about me. Naturally. So he's coming.'

At this, Colonel Akif called over his subordinate and conferred with her *sotto voce* in Turkish.

'He told me not to let anyone know he was coming,' she continued. 'Not to speak of it to anyone. But now I've told you.—Oh, Trevor, I'm sorry!'

Trevor smiled grimly, and shook his head as if to say it couldn't be helped.

'I never thought he'd come!' she whispered. 'I didn't expect that!'

'Never mind.'

'I wish I'd never phoned!' said Carey, bitterly.

'You had to.' He seated himself and briefly took her hand. 'You did the right thing.' Dammit! he thought. Dammit to hell!

Akif now seemed ebullient. He propelled himself forward and vigorously stubbed out his cigarette. 'I am delighted your husband is coming, Mrs Signorello. He could be a great help to me.'

'A help?'

Her surprise seemed to amuse him. 'When does he arrive?'

'Tomorrow.'

'When exactly? and where?—The airport here in Istanbul, of course.'

'He said the evening. His secretary booked the flight while he was on the phone to me. I think he said 8.30. On Turkish Airlines from London.'

'Good.' Akif sat back once more and considered this. 'So, he is coming to your rescue, coming to take you away from all this unpleasantness. That is admirable, I think. Admirable. Noble. How fortunate you are to have such a husband.' Glancing quickly from one to the other of them, he added: 'Even though his coming just now might not be altogether convenient for you both. Ah, well.—And you are to meet him at the airport, Mrs Signorello?'

'No.'

'Ah, you are *not* to meet him at the airport.'

'He said not to. He's concerned about me. He thought it might still be dangerous for me. In fact he made me promise to stay in the hotel until he got there.'

'What hotel?—Not where you are now, obviously.'

'The Pera Palas. His secretary was reserving a room.'

'The Pera Palas. Of course.'

Much as he deplored the notion of Mario, Trevor mentally thanked him for occupying the Colonel's thoughts in place of himself. Akif was now dialing a number on the telephone at his elbow. While he talked, a second subordinate appeared, placed a folder on his desk, and stood waiting at an obsequious distance. The telephone conversation lasted some time, the conversation which followed, between Akif and his subordinate, their heads together over the open folder, even longer. When at last the Colonel looked up it was with a smile of satisfaction. 'Excuse me for neglecting you, my friends! Thank you for your patience.'

'About what I told you—' Trevor began.

'I reserve judgement. We must wait a little.—Now, I may seem merely to place myself safely and boringly on the side of convention and morality, but I have some interest in seeing to it that you, Mrs Signorello, obey your husband like a good wife. You must do as he says, install yourself at once in the room he has so considerately arranged for you at the Pera Palas and await his arrival; while you, Dr Malcolm, must simply stay clear. I suspect Mrs Signorello scarcely wishes to be seen in your company on her husband's arrival, but you must stay clear in any case. Measures will be taken to ensure that this advice is not forgotten by either of you.—Now, if you would be so kind as to wait here with me, Dr Malcolm, my colleague will conduct Mrs Signorello to a typewriter in the next room, on which she will take down certain information.'

Carey had only time to exchange a questioning glance with Trevor before being escorted out.

'She won't be long?' he inquired.

The Colonel smiled and shook his head.

'Well,' exclaimed Trevor with aggressive satisfaction, after a pause. 'You seem to have lost interest in me, at any rate.—do you still think I'm something other than an archaeologist? That I go around killing off people before you can learn something from them? What the hell do you—or did you—think I was?'

Akif laughed shortly and lit another cigarette. 'Before I knew the identity of your victim in Ephesus—that is to say, before I'd had a full report from the agent I'd placed in Selçluk (a man who followed you from there, by the way, but lost you on your walk here, from the ship), I thought you might be working for the Greeks.'

'What!'

'And why not?—This very week, as no doubt you know, we were almost at war. They are our bitter rivals for tourism, among other things. A young industry, here, tourism—on which we place great hope for economic recovery. In fact, without tourism there can be no economic recovery. The Greeks like to portray us as a barbaric and dangerous country. We will take market share from them. Imagine their satisfaction in being able to say that even in what is probably Turkey's most celebrated tourist attraction, the Great Theatre at Ephesus, a tourist is not safe.'

It was a thought Trevor himself had once had. 'But—'

The other held up his hand. 'However, I changed my mind about you when I learned the identity of the dead man at Ephesus.'

Trevor shifted impatiently while Akif suffered a brief coughing spell. 'It's the smoking, Colonel. You're all chimneys in this country.'

'I know, I know.—Well, as I say, I changed my mind about you when I learned the identity of the dead man.'

'Oh?'

'Dr Malcolm, we the military are putting an end to the troubles in our country. The assassinations of politicians, the terrorist attacks on civilians, and so on. All Turks are grateful. However, outsiders do not completely understand. Our friends in NATO, and especially the Americans. The Americans are impatient and want democracy restored at once, instantly—that is to say, prematurely. They have no conception of the traditional role of the military in restoring order here from time to time, restoring order and then bowing out. They think we are like the military dictators of Latin American countries, but we are not. We have not that ambition. But the Americans do not understand that. They make no distinction and seek opportunities to have us discredited.'

'I don't see where I fit into all this.'

'Dr Malcolm, there have been one or two incidents, since the take-over, that have come to light and drawn criticism—justified criticism, once or twice, I will admit. The incident at Ephesus could have been one too many. Scrutiny and publication would have entailed exposure of criminal elements in our official midst. Pressure could have been brought to bear on us, the military, to step down—step down before our task of restoring order and getting the country back to normality is complete.'

You thought I might have been sent here by the Americans? To kill Gokalp, then Merlana.'

'Yes.'

'In the hope that an investigation would follow and the world would find out the two of them were cosily in bed with both the Tourist Police and the Mafia, and that you, the army, had done bugger all about it!'

'Precisely. If you choose to put it thus, crudely.—And were you not sent here by the Americans?—The funding, American—the National Geographic Society an adequate cover—your friend, Mrs Signorello, an American. You see I am still not sure about you, Dr Malcolm. We shall see—'

The arrival of Carey dissuaded him from completing the sentence. He rose instead, and led them both back through the labyrinth of corridors to the main door of the building. 'Upon reaching your room tomorrow, Mrs Signorello,' he said, 'your husband will receive a telephone call from us. Arrangements to meet conveniently, discreetly, will be explained to him.'

'You're going to talk to Mario?"

'Of course. He comes fortuitously. Who better to corroborate your view of events? Besides, I share his interest in *objets d'art*, icons, jewel-encrusted daggers and that sort of thing—and the people who illegally traffic in these when they are part of our national heritage.'

He bade them good night and left them to be escorted by two soldiers to the waiting car.

In the four or five minutes before their arrival at the Pera Palas, Carey and Trevor sought to make sense of what was happening. They faced the prospect of immediate and totally unprepared for separation. Time was to be denied them. Hurriedly, Carey explained that Akif's subordinate had merely taken down details concerning Mario: a physical description, his present address and telephone number, and so on. She recounted the telephone conversation with her husband. If only she hadn't made it!—But Mario's resolve to come to her rescue had taken her completely by surprise. It was the last thing she'd expected. She still couldn't understand it. She'd tried her best to dissuade him. She'd told him the danger was past, that the military were looking after her and she was sure that with their help she would be able to slip out of the country. He'd said he'd better come anyway. In ascribing the attempts on her life to the vengefulness of those he'd had business dealings with, she had underlined the fact that he would be placing his own life at risk; but this had, if anything, merely strengthened his resolve. He blamed himself, told her how responsible he felt, how bitterly he now regretted having let her come to Turkey; but he'd thought nothing of it, that unfortunate business. He'd considered it over and done with.

Trevor listened, while desperately preoccupied with the problem of keeping in touch. Refusing to give up the idea of meeting, he seized on disguise, then bribery, before rejecting both—the first as farcical, the second as unlikely to work with these new military types. He considered creating some distraction at the hotel, but a vision of alert and lethally armed soldiers made him drop this more quickly than the first two ideas.

They drew up before the ornate façacde of the Pera Palas.

'I'll phone,' cried Trevor, as Carey was taken from him. 'I'll phone in an hour or so. They'll give me the number at the desk. We'll work out something. It can't just end like this—'

## Chapter 17

TREVOR COULD BARELY contain his anger and frustration. Waiting in the road outside the Hotel Sahinlar for the car which had dropped him to be swallowed by the darknes, he cursed Akif. How dare the man separate the two of them like this, step in to deny Carey and himself these last precious hours together! He'd counted on dinner with her tonight, a chance to talk things over after this eventful day—to plan, or failing her consent to that, then at least to say goodbye properly. He had no idea what, if anything, could have been arranged between them; what he could have got her to agree to, considering the loyalty she had expressed for her irreproachable husband. He had not even considered how far, in the circumstances, his own conscience would have allowed him to press her to carry on in any form with him. He started walking towards the din of traffic on Ordu Caddesi, wanting to see if that would bring back the men in the car, or prompt others to spring from behind trees or bushes in the narrow strip of park that ran opposite the hotel.

An opportunity to talk would not have changed anything, he was forced, miserably, to admit. Another night with her in his arms would not have changed anything. Or a month of such nights. She was someone else's wife. Still, he was filled with bitter anger at being shoved unexpectedly to the sidelines like this, deprived of all initiative, rendered helpless, by Akif. His strongest urge was to bolt for the Pera Palas; once there, however, he would be seized and locked away by Akif's men, rendered even more helpless than he was now.

From Akif"s unexpected and cruel decree, he turned his thoughts to Mario. He cursed Mario equally—for deciding to intervene, for choosing to arrive when the danger was past, for coming to snatch Carey from him; Carey whose life he, Trevor, had twice saved!

Walking on, he took several deep breaths of the coal-smoke filled night air and told himself what a fool he was. Apparently, he had fallen in love with Carey—if that is what having come to want, to need, her, amounted to. He was doubly a fool now for fulminating against what was, after all, the perfectly predictable and irreproachable behaviour of the husband and the policeman. Akif was a professional, understandably concerned with the task in hand, only doing his duty. And Mario was a normal husband, who, hearing from his wife that there had been trouble, had instantly decided to come to be with her. Just what any caring husband would have done. And beyond this, in Mario's case if was commendable—assuming there to be truth in Carey's conviction that by coming he would be placing his own life in danger. No, he could not, in justice, blame Mario for coming.

Further, he ruefully reflected, he had Mario to thank for saving him from further scrutiny by the Colonel; possibly with unpleasant consequences. A misinterpretation with potentially ugly repercussions. Brought under discussion by Carey halfway through the interview, the husband had clearly come to interest Colonel Akif more than the lover.

Dwelling on Akif's line of questioning during the second part of the interview, the way in which, after listening to Carey, he had seemed to abandon them both for Mario, Trevor found himself puzzled. He was moved to reconstruct the scene in Akif's office. Why had Carey been called away to supply information on Mario, and what had the Colonel and his aide to say to one another while bent over that folder? Did it have to do with what happened on Mario's last visit to Turkey? Something Akif had flung off towards the end of their interview in his office sprang to mind; something about *people who illegally traffic in jewel-encrusted daggers and so on, when they're part of our national heritage.* Was Mario doing this? Siphoning off priceless bits of the national heritage? Trevor's spirits rose with the notion, and rose higher as he imagined Mario doing time in a Turkish prison. To this picture was soon added another, however: that of Carey, the loyal wife, visiting regularly, and like 'Patience on a Monument,' waiting out the husband's term.

Approaching the glare, the noise and commotion of the still flowing crowds and vehicles on Ordu Caddesi, he turned back. It was already after ten. He had told Carey he would phone. So much had happened, and in so short a time. The galling thing was, he had nothing to say to her—nothing that would help their situation, at least.

Directing his gaze along the unreliably lighted road towards the hotel entrance, he thought he saw a figure crouching between two parked cars. One of Akif's men after all? The thought of knocking him to the pavement, putting up some sort of fight, came as a welcome, if unrealistic, one. On reaching the spot he found no one, however. Walking on, he came abreast of Roxelana's Chrysler. He was thinking about her now for the first time since the *fracas* with Merlana and the soldier in the square. Preoccupied, he supposed, first with his own defence, then with Carey's intervention and Akif's unexpected reaction to it, he'd not got round to mentioning her to the Colonel. He asked himself if Roxelana's still being at large represented a continuance of danger for Carey? Surely not. The military were protecting her at the Pera Palas. Anyway, Roxelana could have no knowledge of what Akif had decreed, no knowledge of Carey's being now at the Pera Palas.

His fingers closed on the keys to the Chrysler, still in his pocket. At the same moment a voice came out of the darkness, telling him not to move.

'I have a knife,' came the voice.

He recognised the voice: the deep, throaty, smoker's voice, the voice of Roxelana. His stomach churned. He had taken her car; he had assisted in the death of her colleague. He expected to feel the knife in his back.

'You left the door unlocked. Open it and get in. Move over to the driver's seat.'

He tried to reassure himself that she wouldn't kill him—not there and then, at least. No, she was going to make him drive her somewhere, and then do it. He thought of hurling the keys out the half open window, but the next moment felt her scrabbling in his jacket pocket and taking them. Turning, to find her looking fixedly at him, he dropped his eyes. Her hands lay in her lap. He saw no knife. But then his head was jerked back by a blow. His hand flew to his burning cheek: she had managed, with the speed of a lioness, to swivel where she was and slap his face.

'It was not nice, what you did,' she said with sullen emphasis. 'I do not like that. You are involved after all with American woman. You said you did not want that, but you did.'

Her words left him astonished—the words, and the hurt tone, of a jilted woman, rather than a single-mindedly professional killer.

'It was not nice,' she repeated sulkily.

He pounced on the one thing in his favour. 'Look, Roxelana, I've just been grilled by a fellow called Akif, Colonel Akif—of Military Intelligence.—You know of him? Well, never mind.—The point is, *I didn't say a word about you*. Understand?—Not a word!'

Roxelana stared straight ahead of her without speaking.

'Really; I made no mention of you. Otherwise his men would've waited here for you to collect your car, wouldn't they?'

She frowned, appeared to weigh this. 'You say nothing about me?—I am glad.'

'I'm sorry about your friend,' he faltered.

'Not my friend.'

'Not—?'

'I work with him sometimes, like the other. It doesn't matter.' She turned slightly, rested her enormous eyes on him. 'I don't care.'

'I'm glad.'

'It is a shame you did not want to make love with me. You make fun of me, instead.'

This, he had not expected. 'I—'

She heaved a long wheezy sigh, and repeated: 'It is a shame.'

Could the woman really have minded? A stunned silence fell on him, which at length he judged it wise to break. 'I deceived you. But I couldn't do anything else just then. You must understand. Too much on my plate.'

'You made the fool of me—'

He spluttered a protest.

'I believed you.'

'Roxelana, what I said was true, about wanting an Eastern woman. And about finding you … attractive.'

'Coincidentally, I look for a Western man. It is pity—' She lit a cigarette, inhaled deeply and waited a few seconds before directing a small cloud of pungent smoke at the closed window beside her. 'And why is your American friend not here? What have you done with her?'

'She's … away just now.'

Roxelana laughed harshly. 'You need not worry. I would not hurt her. That is finished.'

Trevor hid his relief. 'It's finished between the two of us, too.'

'Oh?'

'Yes, it's finished for the two of us—because her husband is coming to reclaim her.'

'Her husband? Her husband, Mario Signorello—' The corners of her rubbery mouth twitched up in a brief smile. 'Then it is finished *for her*,' she breathed, and looked away.

For her? Finished for her?—The remark made no sense, yet it chilled him.

'You did not tell the Colonel about me,' turning abruptly and looking hard at him. 'And you will not—'

'No, I didn't. And I won't.—Roxelana, what exactly did you mean by "finished for her"?'

'If you were to tell him, tell the Colonel,' she continued, 'others would come for you.—So, you no longer have the American woman.'

His eyes were drawn to her long many-ringed fingers as they opened the glove compartment. He half expected a revolver. Instead he saw her tear off part of a brown envelope, take a ballpoint from her bag, and write something. The torn-off fragment she then slipped into the side pocket of his jacket.

'But it is no good,' she spat out abruptly. 'I am stupid!'

'What—?'

Trembling visibly, she said with some ferocity: 'Go now! Go—!'

In need of no further urging, he opened the car door and scrambled out. He stood in the road, dazed; watching the tail lights of the Chrysler until they disappeared in the night.

*Her husband? Ah... it is finished, then. Finished for her!* Roxelana's words rang in his head, making sinister sense, and propelling him to the Hotel Sahinlar and up to his room, where he wasted no time in telephoning the desk and asking to be connected with the Pera Palas. He must first make her believe what he believed. He might have it all wrong but couldn't risk ignoring the import of what Roxelana had said. He must warn Carey, alert her, so she could tell Akif—in case he imagined Mario's misdemeanours stopped short of murder.

It soon became clear that he could not do so, however: calls to Mrs Signorello's room were not allowed through just now, the receptionist at the Pera Palas cheerfully informed him.

It was late; the Colonel would not still be in his office. Trevor tugged the Istanbul telephone directory to the floor from the bedside table and knelt over the 'A's: thirteen Akifs, none of them designated 'Colonel.' Fuming, he dialled—working through the numbers and rousing six Akifs before recognising the voice of the seventh.

'I take it you now accept Mrs Signorello's story that Gokalp and Merlana were hired to kill her?' he asked, after some introductory explanation.

'I prefer not to comment just at present.'

'They *were* hired to kill her, and I'm damn sure you know it!'

'Dr Malcolm, it is late.'

'You said this Gokalp and Merlana were in the Mafia *and* the Police, right?'

'And you said you had something important to ask me—'

'Yes, I want to know if you have any idea who hired them—because I have. His name is Mario Signorello!'

There followed a pause; then: 'That may be, Dr Malcolm. I am not in a position to comment on the domestic affairs of Mr and Mrs Signorello.'

'You showed some interest in him.'

'For reasons of my own, yes.'

'What better reason than that he wants people killed?'

An audible sigh. 'You are naïve, Dr Malcolm.'

'*What better reason*?'

'Dr Malcolm, please understand … understand that for more than a year I have worked to discover the identities of certain members of the Anatolian Tourist Police who are connected with organized crime in this country, individuals corrupted under the *ancien régime* and carrying on their activities in the teeth of our new dispensation. If they are not found, then contagion from them will spread, things will be as bad as before, and we of the Military will be discredited. This would suit the Americans. I explained to you how eager the Americans are to have us step down. I learned about Merlana and Gokalp, and would have trapped one or the other into supplying me with names of their more highly placed colleagues. I and my department would then have been in a position to clean out the lot of them. Now, thanks to you and your friend, I find myself obliged to give up that line of inquiry—and pursue another.'

'Yes—'

'Indeed. I expect much from Mario Signorello. I have been set back once; I do not intend to be set back again. I shan't lose this most fortuitous opportunity. I do not intend to sacrifice the larger advantage to some merely personal concerns of yours.'

'What are you going to do when he arrives tomorrow morning?'

'A room close to theirs has been specially prepared, to which he will be summoned shortly after his arrival. In that specially prepared room we shall talk. That is all.'

'About—?'

'About certain of his activities during previous visits to Turkey. Particularly his last.'

'You think he's guilty of something.'

'I *know* he is guilty of something. Something rather large.'

'He'll go to prison, then?'

'Oh, I think not, Dr Malcolm. That would be a rash move on our part. Do not forget what passport he holds. He is an American. I count on his accepting my terms. And charges will be dropped, you understand—as soon as he has supplied me with the information I require.'

'You're doing a deal—'

'But of course.'

'Names—'

'Precisely.'

'You're saying you won't act to prevent him murdering his wife? You're going to let him go—even if it means her being left dead in their room at the Pera Palas?'

'No, no. Calm yourself, Dr Malcolm. Rest assured, he will not be so foolish as to do that, knowing we are nearby. Rest assured that we take responsibility for her safety while in this country.'

Trevor felt reassured; then it occurred to him to ask: 'But what happens when you've got your names from him? What happens when you've got your precious information?'

'In exchange, Mario Signorello will be free. On the understanding that he leaves the country and does not return.'

'Leaves the country?—*but he'll take her with him*!'

'Is he not her husband?' Akif calmly rejoined. 'Mrs Signorello mentioned to my assistant his intention of taking her to Greece—'

'*Greece*!—It would just suit you if he murdered her there, wouldn't it?'

This was met with silence.

'Greece would be great, wouldn't it? Ideal for you! Preferably on the Acropolis—damage to *their* tourist industry, perhaps—!'

Trevor heard a polite 'Good-night,' after which the line went dead. He sat staring into space, turning over and over in his mind the words of Colonel Akif. Mario hadn't succeeded in having his wife murdered, but he was to be given another chance—by Akif, Colonel Akif the military policeman, who cared only about his deal, only about the names of Gokalp's and Merlana's superiors, and the others. He got to his feet and strode to the door with the intention of opening it, only to return to his place beside the telephone.

Moments later his fingers closed on the torn strip of envelope in the pocket of his jacket. Unfolding it he read the telephone number Roxelana had written there. Between the sporadic foghorns of ships lying at anchor offshore in the Sea of Marmara he could hear his own heart beating fast. He lifted the telephone receiver and dialed; and then, after the briefest of conversations, fetched his jacket and left the room.

## Chapter 18

A PRISONER IN her room the following evening, Carey awaited agitatedly the knock that would announce the arrival of her husband. It must come at any moment; his plane had been due to land an hour ago. At each set of footsteps in the corridor she prepared herself anew. Several times she had rehearsed how she would receive him, what she would say; and several times revised or rejected it. She saw she must mention Trevor. But she was cruelly torn between admitting and not admitting to loving him, between explaining how her resolve not to become involved with him had crumbled, and admitting only to having been thrown together with him and forced to accept his help. Before this difficulty, and the effort she envisaged merely in greeting Mario with some semblance of warmth, in thanking him for coming, in seeming grateful for this rescue, her heart sank. The lack of spontaneity, of sincerity, of truth, that would be in the denial of loving Trevor, dismayed her.

How had she allowed herself to fall in love with Trevor? She'd never imagined it possible. Could anything have been farther from her thoughts, anything more improbable? Only two of three days ago she'd told herself how glad she would be to see the last of him. It had taken her by surprise, this love—stormed her heart, ambushed mind and body. Perhaps it would pass; perhaps it would be over as quickly as it had come.

Having not heard from Trevor, she had tried to phone him—only to be told that for the time being she could neither make calls nor receive them. The time being was to be wasted, then. And now, at any moment, the knock would come, the knock that would say: You are not to see him again, you are not even to be allowed a parting word, a kiss.

Ill prepared though she had thought herself, the knock, when it came, brought the violent certainty that she would confess everything and take the consequences. She loved Trevor. Against her will it had happened, and in spite of everything. She loved him and would declare it. Yet a shiver of fear ran through her, a new fear of Mario; a fear mysteriously engendered by a coldness in the tone of his voice over the phone, which belied all the concern his words carried. Could he have learned of her leaving the tour, of her meeting someone else? The indifference he had shown towards her of late could not be counted on to help her. He was too full of himself, too accustomed to having his own way. And too sure of her compliance. Her legs seemed ready to collapse beneath her as she walked to the door.

The next moment she felt as though she had been flung backwards by some physical force, an explosion or a blow—for there stood, *not Mario, but Trevor*!

'It's all right,' he said, taking her in his arms after closing the door. 'It's all right.' He spoke without elation, and held her for several seconds without letting her go.

'But the soldiers, Akif—and Mario!' she protested breathlessly.

'I've cleared it with Akif. He's downstairs. He knows I'm here.'

'Knows—'

'In fact … he sent me.'

'Sent you!'—She pushed away from him, freed herself entirely, to stare into his face in amazement.

'Asked me to come, in fact. Asked me to tell you what's happened.'

The colour had drained from her face. 'Trevor, tell me! What has happened?'

He tried to pull her to him again, to hide his face over her shoulder, but she resisted. 'It's Mario—'

'They've put him in prison—'

He hesitated, dropped his eyes from hers.

'I don't care if they have,' she hurried hectically on. 'I just don't care, Trevor. Not at all! Understand that I don't! In fact—'

He looked up. 'Carey, no. It's not prison—'

'Not,' she echoed uncomprehendingly.

'No. He's been shot. Killed, in fact.'

She pulled in her breath sharply.

'Getting into a taxi at the airport,' he continued quietly. 'Someone shot him. From a motorcycle.'

She reeled dizzily from him and collapsed onto a couch beside the window. Her thoughts were her own, tumbling in on her, racing past like debris in a swollen river. She must seize what she could, put them together. Her husband was dead. Mario was no more. She must understand that. Well, she needn't tell him anything now. Not ever.—But why was she not sorry? Why could she feel nothing? She was shocked, astonished, scarcely able to believe. Yet she was not sorry. For this she ought to reproach herself. Wasn't she responsible? That phone call. He would still be alive if she hadn't telephoned him and let him know she was in danger. I'm *not* to blame, she tried to tell herself.—Yet her heart misgave. He'd decided instantly to come! He knew it was dangerous, and yet he'd risked his life for her!—Still, that wasn't what she'd expected, his deciding to drop everything and come to Turkey for her sake. She couldn't have foreseen that. There was no need for him to come, was there? She'd explained that she could leave the country on her own now and be safe. She'd tried to make him believe there was no need for him to come.

Aware of an alien joy encroaching on her confusion, a flood of happiness lapping closer, she fought to fend it off. The effort made her cry at last.

'I know,' Trevor broke in. 'Of course, it's a shock. Bound to be. Even though—well, he was you husband—'

'It's not that,' she moaned. 'I can't explain.'

'Listen,' he continued gently. 'I know how you must feel, but there's something else—'

She smiled up at him, weakly, lovingly. 'There's always something else, isn't there? With you?'

'Carey—'

'But no, no!' she murmured, sobbing and shaking her head. 'You *don't* know how I feel. You can't.—I'm *glad*! That's the wretched thing about it! And I'm ashamed, ashamed for being glad, for not being more sorry. For not being sorry at all!—And I don't know why. It's not what I would've expected of myself.'

He seized on this. 'Don't be!' he exclaimed. 'Don't be sorry! Leave that to the Colonel. *He's* sorry all right. In fact he's furious. But sorry is the very last thing you should be!'

She dabbed her cheek with a handkerchief and stared questioningly up at him.

'—Because it was him all along! *He arranged it.* It was Mario, your Mario!'

'What are you saying!' She sat upright, and away from him.

'You blamed the Turks.' He spoke rapidly now. 'You thought it was them wanting to get back at Mario for something. But it was him!' He flung himself beside her. 'Whatever it was he told you, about making enemies here, was rubbish. He may have cheated someone, had some trouble over it, but his real reason for not wanting to come back and do business was that that business was no longer possible under the new military regime! It involved exporting works of art to America, works that went smoothly through the hands of a well-organised ring of thieves and corrupt police and customs officials. The military take-over made that too dangerous, impossible in fact.'

Carey seemed not to understand.

'He hired those characters! He wanted you dead. He hired Gokalp and Merlana!'

She remained in shocked silence for a full minute.

Trevor rose, went to the window, stood with his back to her looking out at the night.

'I can't believe it!' she murmured at last, shaking her head. 'How could I not have known, never have suspected?'

He returned to her. 'I'm afraid it's true.'

Remaining seated, she rocked silently for a time. 'Odd, to think I imagined that he showed concern; but … you're saying … he was coming only to kill me.'

'I'd say so. Since the others had failed.'

'I thought I knew him. But I had no idea … no inkling of what he was really like, what he was capable of.'

He nodded.

'Even after seven years—'

'But you know why it suited him to have you dead, don't you?' he said, frowning. 'You know the reason, the motive—'

She got up slowly and faced him.

'Carey, you know why he did it!—You know what I'm talking about. Well; out with it.'

'Money,' she said with a sigh. 'Of course, money. Insurance, stocks.'

He nodded, shook his head, a grim smile of satisfaction pursing his lips. 'The root of all evil.'

'Isn't it always that?' she said. 'Not generosity after all, those investments he made for me! The times he would top up my bank account, suggest ways the money he'd put there could be made to work for more.'—And wasn't that at least partly why I married him? she added silently.

'Money!' Trevor echoed her, spitting the word out with some vehemence.

'I suppose he was in difficulties, financial difficulties. Worse than I imagined. Now I understand why.'

'So it occurred to him—'

'I've always had my own investment portfolio and he's had his. We have different brokers but he knew what I had. Our wills are identical: on the death of one or the other of us the assets go to the survivor. The same with the money for our life insurance policies—'

'Winner takes all.'

She nodded unsmilingly. 'But Trevor, who shot him? Those enemies he talked about? Do the police know?'

'Not enemies, but friends. Those connections Mario had here. One of them, at least; who wanted him dead because he would have revealed their names to Colonel Akif in exchange for Akif's dropping charges and letting him leave the country.'

She considered this, then frowned. 'I wonder how they found out, these friends, or this friend. And so quickly. That Mario was coming, I mean. The plane—the arrival time—everything. Who could have told them?'

He took several paces back and forth before replying. 'Carey, there was something I never explained. Didn't have time … The day we met I mentioned to you that I'd noticed in the parking lot at Ephesus what I thought was a young man, a youth in a beret and dark glasses. This individual was talking to a boy—come to think of it, probably the boy who brought the message to Kadir to say the tour bus should leave without waiting for you. Well, that was no young man.' He told her of his encounter with Roxelana when he'd fled from the Hilton with the passport; of Roxelana's waylaying him at the café, of her receiving the phone call from Merlana, and of his theft of her car, and afterwards of his having forgotten to mention her existence to Colonel Akif. Encountering Roxelana a second time, when dropped by Akif's men outside the Sahinlar late last night, he'd managed to convince her he hadn't given her name to the Colonel. Something she'd said on parting had alerted him to Mario's having been behind the whole thing. Later, convinced that Akif was only interested in gaining information from Mario, and that he wouldn't lift a finger to protect Carey once she was out of the country, he'd resorted to disclosing to Roxelana the fact that Mario was arriving and that Akif planned a deal with him: freedom from arrest for past misdemeanours in exchange for the names of his contacts here in Turkey. 'I knew there was no way Roxelana was going to allow Mario to spill all those beans,' he concluded.

Carey thought for a moment, then raised her eyes to his and said slowly, wonderingly: 'Your telling this woman, this Roxelana, meant … certain death for him, for Mario—'

'I—'

'You knew that, knew Mario would be killed once you told her.'

He nodded, barely able to return her gaze.

She hesitated, sighed, shook her head. 'So, really, it was you. You, who killed him.—But then, I think I always knew you would.'

'Carey!—but that's nonsense!'

'And I, who set out wanting to change—in one sense or another,' she reflected quietly, more to herself than to him. 'The woman, Gyges's queen, in it from the start—unconsciously, half consciously.'

'Carey, I don't follow. What's this about a queen?'

'Nothing.' She swung around, smiling and shaking her head, to face him. 'What the hell am I doing in the company of a man who's been responsible, directly or indirectly, for the violent deaths of three men in less than a week? Three men, *and one of them my husband*!'

He laughed uncertainly. 'All in a good cause—.'

'My bodyguard! And now the kingdom!'

He had no idea what she was talking about, but felt relief, having half expected the loyal wife in her to resurface and say she would never speak to him again. Instead, he felt her arms go round his neck, her lips on his.

'I remember your saying it's impossible to know someone completely,' she continued, with her face against his. 'I sure struck out on Mario, but I'm beginning to think you'd be even more of a challenge.'

'Hell no, I'm an open book.'

'Odd, isn't it?' she mused, breaking from him. 'My husband paid someone a lot of money to have me killed, and failed. You had my husband killed, without spending anything.'

Trevor, thinking of the night he'd ended up having to spend with Roxelana, merely smiled.

* * * * *

There was to be no war after all, between Turkey and Greece.

It struck Carey, journeying to the airport with Trevor after a day of hectic and irksome arrangements, that Istanbul seemed indifferent to the fact—as though too old to care, too jaded to rejoice or repine.

It was still early but the strength of the spring sun promised a day of heat. She noticed trailing above the roofs of passing houses only the thinnest of coal smoke clouds. Traffic was still too light to drown out the songs of birds or the banter of shopkeepers rolling down awnings and setting out their wares. The car coming to a halt before the terminal building, she wondered if the soldiers posted on either side of the sliding doors had been there when Mario arrived. If so, they hadn't been vigilant enough to bring down the motorcyclist.

Consequently here Carey was, travelling back to the States with the body of her husband.

Inside the building, rejoining Trevor after lining up at the check-in counter, she remarked: 'All I care about is getting everything at home settled and hurrying back here—you know that, my Darling.'

'To marry me, I suppose you're thinking.' There was mischief in his eyes. 'You know how I hate calculation.'

'To marry you?' she flashed merrily. 'Marry again? And so soon? Are you kidding?' She stood on tip-toe and kissed him lightly. 'No, but I would like to see this Aphrodisias of yours. That's really all I'm interested in.'

'Ah—'

'It's too late for me to become an archaeologist,' she went on with a theatrical sigh, 'a real archaeologist. I'd like to do some digging, though, get dirt under my fingernails, see what it's like, your sort of life, the sort of life I might have had.—I can't think of anything more exciting than finding one of those terra cotta heads or part of a statue!—So you'll take me on, when I come back?'

'Well—' he looked down, scuffed the floor.

'As a volunteer. No pay. I wouldn't want money. I've got too much of that now.'

'Too much of it? Have you really?' He betrayed some interest.

'Of course. All mine and all Mario's too. Winner takes all, as you put it. I'm as rich as that fellow we talked about in Selçuk.'

'Croesus.'

'That's him.—But it's the root of all evil, as you say. So I'll probably give most of it away.'

There came a pause before he resumed with: 'That strikes me as … a wee bit rash.'

'Oh?'

'Aye, just a tad.'

'Uh huh.'

'Well,' he coughed. 'You should never despise money, good money, you know.' He stood a little aloof, frowning and stroking his chin.

The announcement sounded, in Turkish and in English, for passengers to board the aircraft which was to take Carey on the first leg of her return journey to the States.

'Well, I'm off. Thanks again for everything—dinners, getting my passport, and today my suitcase, and of course saving my life at least twice. But no, you mustn't think I'm coming back here with any idea of marrying you. It's much too soon. I hardly know you, and judging by my last performance that might take some time.'

'After seven years of marriage you want seven without, is that it? Seven fat with your last, seven lean unmarried to me.'

'Not lean for me! But no, try me again before that. Before seven. Just for fun—'

'In the course of digging, perhaps?'

'That would be a good time.'

'It all depends—'

'Depends?'

'On how well you get on with the digging, and—'

'And,'

'Well, a wee contribution might ensure that you have a place to dig.'

'Ah, a contribution to the Save Aphrodisias Fund?'

'Aye!'

'I'll think about it.' She laughed and kissed him; then turned and fled through the doors marked Passengers Only.

ISBN 141209146-2

9 781412 091466